Advance Praise

"Written with heart, depth, and pace, Hirahara's sixth case is hard to put down."

— *Kirkus Reviews*

"Mas Arai is a wholly original sleuth—reluctant, curmudgeonly, and irresistible. In *Sayonara Slam*, he delves into baseball, World War II, and the complex history between Japan and Korea, all while grappling with that most enduring mystery: love. Naomi Hirahara has created a story that's both meaningful and great fun; you'll be cheering until the very last play."

— Nina Revoyr, author of *Lost Canyon*, *Southland*, and *Wingshooters*

"Another compelling Mas Arai murder mystery, this time framed through the game of baseball. With reference to the early days of the sport in Japan via Babe Ruth's visit in 1934 and the internment leagues begun in the American desert behind barbed wire by Kenichi Zenimura, the story climaxes in the contemporary confines of Dodger Stadium. The unraveling of the clues to the murder puts a new spin on an old pastime."

— Terry Cannon, executive director of the Baseball Reliquary

Praise for the Mas Arai Mysteries

"A shrewd sense of character and a formidable narrative engine."

—Chicago Tribune

"Naomi Hirahara's well-plotted, wholesome whodunit offers a unique look at L.A.'s Japanese American community, with enough twists and local flavor to keep you guessing till the end."

— Entertainment Weekly

"In author Hirahara's deft hands (she's an Edgar winner), the human characters, especially Mas, always make for a compelling read."

— Mystery Scene

"This perfectly balanced gem deserves a wide readership."

— Publishers Weekly

"A compelling grasp of the Japanese American sub-culture...absolutely fascinating."

— Asian American Press

"Hirahara has a keen eye for the telling detail and an assured sense of character."

— Los Angeles Times

More Mas Arai Mysteries

Strawberry Yellow
Blood Hina
Snakeskin Shamisen
Gasa-Gasa Girl
Summer of the Big Bachi

More Fiction by Naomi Hirahara

Grave on Grand Avenue (an Ellie Rush mystery)
Murder on Bamboo Lane (an Ellie Rush mystery)
1001 Cranes

Selected Nonfiction by Naomi Hirahara

A Scent of Flowers:
The History of the Southern California Flower Market

Silent Scars of Healing Hands:
Oral Histories of Japanese American Doctors
in World War II Detention Camps

An American Son:
The Story of George Arataki, Founder of Mikasa and Kenwood

Green Makers:
Japanese American Gardeners in Southern California

Naomi Hirahara

PROSPECT
·PARK·
BOOKS

Published by Prospect Park Books
2359 Lincoln Avenue
Altadena, California 91001
www.prospectparkbooks.com

PROSPECT
·PARK·
BOOKS

Distributed by Consortium Book Sales & Distribution
www.cbsd.com

Library of Congress Cataloging in Publication Data
Names: Hirahara, Naomi, 1962- author.
Title: Sayonara slam / Naomi Hirahara.
Description: Altadena, California : Prospect Park Books, [2016] | Series: A
  Mas Arai mystery ; 6
Identifiers: LCCN 2015050666 (print) | LCCN 2016005763 (ebook) |
ISBN 9781938849732 (acid-free paper) | ISBN 9781938849749 ()
Subjects: LCSH: Murder--Investigation--Fiction. | Japanese
  Americans--Fiction. | Gardeners--Fiction. | Baseball stories. | BISAC:
  FICTION / Mystery & Detective / General. | GSAFD: Mystery fiction.
Classification: LCC PS3608.I76 S29 2016 (print) | LCC PS3608.I76
(ebook) |
  DDC 813/.6--dc23
LC record available at http://lccn.loc.gov/2015050666

Design & layout by Amy Inouye, Future Studio
Printed in the United States of America

While certain landmarks, such as Dodger Stadium, are real, the stories in this mystery are completely fictional. The World Baseball Classic championship was held at Dodger Stadium in 2009, but the course of events was quite different from those of this novel.

IN MEMORY OF TOBI YAMASAKI AND FRANK EGO

Chapter One

At first, Mas Arai thought it was a bat boy playing some kind of prank. The figure on the mound could not have been much more than five feet tall. But this wasn't a neighborhood park. This was Dodger Stadium, born in 1962 over plowed-down Latino homes and the oldest baseball stadium on the west coast. In two hours, Japan would face archrival South Korea in the 2009 World Baseball Classic. No time for a mischievous youngster to sneak up and pretend he was a baseball *senshu*. Weren't the security guards standing on the sidelines going to put a stop to this nonsense?

There was no doubt about it, Mas's eyes were bad. Haruo, who Mas would never credit as his best friend, first nagged him about it. Then Genessee, whose role in Mas's life was also unspoken, even though they had been together for five years, took over. She had finally driven him to the Costco on her side of town to get a real eye doctor to do a checkup. Mas had resented being forced to recite giant letters on a screen and reading minuscule lines on cards. What fool could see those letters, not to mention one who was nearing eighty years of age?

Genessee had advocated for colorful plastic-framed glasses that Mas had seen young people wearing, but he would have none of that. If he had to wear glasses other than the readers from his local drugstore, he wasn't going to go *majime*, book smart. He'd instead chosen bank-robber cool—tinted gold wire-rimmed ones that actor Steve McQueen might have worn in the heist movie, *The Getaway*.

Mas slipped on his glasses now to make sure he was seeing right. The person on the mound was in uniform, wearing a dark blue shirt with "Japan" in red emblazoned across it. The hair, which stuck out underneath a baseball cap, was a little long for Mas's taste, but at least it didn't look to be streaked blue or purple. He then blinked hard, once and then twice. Sonofagun. The pitcher was a woman.

"That's Neko Kawasaki. Plays on the minor leagues in Hawaii." The voice came from behind him. He turned his head to see an Asian man with a dazzling white head of hair. He wore tinted glasses not unlike Mas's.

"Sheezu any good?" Mas asked. As soon as he said it, he knew it was a stupid question. This was the pros, and not even limited to the United States, so she had to be good.

"She's a knuckleballer. Not too many of them these days. Wakefield might be one of the last ones. " Mas knew about old man Tim Wakefield, a fortysomething Red Soxer for… what, close to fifteen years now?

"I'm Smitty Takaya." The white-haired man extended his right hand.

"Mas. Mas Arai."

"Lloyd's father-in-law. You're a gardener, right?"

Mas widened his eyes. He wasn't used to strangers knowing anything about him before meeting him, and it made him suspicious.

"Maybe you can take a look at our Japanese garden someday."

Mas frowned. Maybe his ears weren't working either. Who ever heard of a Japanese garden in Dodger Stadium?

"One was dedicated out there past the edge of the parking lot. You could draw a line from home plate to center-field and you'll find it out there."

Mas took a second look at the white-haired man. He wore a light-blue polo shirt with the L.A. Dodgers logo prominently embroidered on the left-hand side. Maybe this guy wasn't fooling around. Maybe he was a big shot.

"I work in the front office." Smitty gestured to the upper deck, where enclosed offices overlooked left field. "I process his and the rest of the checks for the staff. Head grounds-keeper, a nice promotion for Lloyd."

It took five years, but Mas's son-in-law was finally making good money.

"He told me you'd be helping us. Good at shaving lawn-mower blades, I hear. *Dozo yoroshiku*," Smitty added in perfect Japanese.

Mas widened his eyes. "You knowsu Japanese. You'zu Kibei?"

"I'm an all-American Buddhahead. From Honolulu. But I played in Japan for the Flyers, now known as the

Nippon-Ham Fighters. They were in Tokyo Dome back then." So he *was* a big shot. The Japanese Baseball League was just getting back on its feet when Mas left Hiroshima in 1947. This Smitty was lucky to be Flyer instead of a Ham Fighter. But whatever he was, Mas was fully impressed. And that rarely occurred, or as his late wife, Chizuko, had said, only the possibility of winning a trifecta would get Mas Arai out of his easy chair on his day off.

"I first came in to help with international scouting after I retired from playing, but then I was always good with numbers, so I slowly moved up the ranks." A thick gold ring with "World Champions" shone from his right hand. "I usually stay in the front office, but I guess they needed my bilingual skills. These fellows from Nihon, they're supposed to study English in school, but their pronunciation is lousy."

Mas's face grew hot, and he looked away. He was born in America and not *Nihon*, the most popular name for Japan by its citizens, but he'd been taken by his family to Hiroshima when he was only three years old. After spending close to fifteen years in Japan, he moved back to the States. Despite being here for sixty years, his language skills were definitely subpar.

They heard curses from Japan's catcher, who was having a terrible time anticipating where the knuckleball pitches would land. Neko Kawasaki had him chasing balls in the dirt by the dugout. Or else the ball would bounce off his chest protector, his glove moving much too late.

The batter wasn't fairing that well, either. A thirtysomething man with dyed yellow hair, the color of burnt hay, he couldn't anticipate the trajectory of the pitch and ended up swinging air.

"She's getting them good. That knuckleball is tricky. I hope these guys will be ready for Jin-Won Kim."

Mas drew a blank, and it must have been plenty obvious from the look on his face.

"He's a pitcher for the Unicorns," Smitty explained. "Yeah, you heard me right, there's a Korean team with that name. I guess me being a former Ham Fighter, I shouldn't talk. But our fans called us the Fighters, okay?" He glared at Mas through his tinted eyeglasses, even though Mas had said nothing out loud.

"It's not about power, you know," Smitty continued. "You don't need for the ball to go fast. It's how you hold the ball with your fingernails." He pulled a baseball out of his pocket and simulated by placing his thumb behind the bottom seam and digging two fingernails right above the top seam. And what was that in the center of the ball—some kind of Japanese chicken scratch?

"Neva seen a girl play," Mas murmured out loud.

"Well, let's not get too far. She's just helping the Japan team prepare for Jin-Won Kim. Kind of like a batting coach, what have you. Most of them have never faced a knuckleball pitcher. He's the closer, the one who comes in at the end and sweeps everything up. And by the way they are hitting, it doesn't look like they're going to fare too well today."

"Dad, is everything okay?" Every time his son-in-law called him Dad, Mas had to do a double take. Lloyd, sunburnt and lean, looked different in his powder-blue polo shirt, khaki shorts, and cap. He wore wraparound sunglasses like he was pretending to be a movie producer instead of a glorified gardener. Mas had always wanted a son, but he'd never imagined this.

Smitty dipped the lip of his cap toward Lloyd. "You have a good father-in-law. He knows his baseball, that's for sure." He then looked toward the sound of voices coming from the other side of the field. A crowd of photographers, mostly Japanese men who were balancing heavy lenses on poles that reminded Mas of black PVC pipe, were jostling for space. "I better see what all that's about."

After Smitty was beyond earshot, Lloyd muttered to Mas, "I hope you didn't say too much to him. Smitty has more influence than you'd think."

Mas gritted the back of his dentures. He hated *oshaberi,* people who moved their traps without saying much of anything, and now his own son-in-law was practically accusing him of being a chatterbox. He didn't know if he liked this version of the giant gardener with his shaven golden locks. Before, Lloyd was a *bura-bura* type who didn't seem to have much ambition or care much what other people thought of him. But now with this fancy title and job, he was suddenly Mr. Sensitive, Mr. Politics. His newfound respectability did buy him and his family a lot more things, Mas had to admit. There was only one problem. In spite of their increased income, they still weren't moving out of Mas's house in Altadena.

His grandson Takeo was now eight, a third-grader at a private school in Pasadena. Mas figured the tuition was why they weren't making a move. And also Mari had returned to her first love, filmmaking. Seemed like everyone in the Arai family was doing the things that they wanted to do. Everyone aside from Mas Arai.

"Whyzu you just tell them they gotta move out," Haruo had said a month ago when they were fixing a sprinkler leak at the home of his daughter, Kiyomi. Haruo had gone to therapy for his gambling addiction for nine months, which apparently made him some kind of expert on things of the heart. He used a mysterious lingo, with words like "codependency" and "boundaries."

Haruo was one to talk. He had an adult stepdaughter, Dee, under his roof as well. But Mas wasn't going to get on his case about Dee. He knew firsthand that most of her life had been a struggle. So he gritted his teeth and sat through Haruo's amateur psychological analysis. Genessee claimed that his friendship with Haruo had made Mas into a good man. Mas had been called a number of things, but never good. To hear it made him feel off-balance, unsteady.

Anyway, what would happen if Mari, Lloyd, and Takeo did move out? It would mean the McNally house would be empty. There'd be room enough for Genessee to move in, although she seemed more than comfortable in her home in Mid-City. And all the things that were unspoken may then have the space to be spoken. Mas preferred a crowded house to that.

He returned his concentration to the Japanese coaches and players, seeing if he recognized any of them. Since they were all wearing the Japan team uniform, they were harder to distinguish from one another. There was the pitcher for the Red Sox with the ridiculous braided necklace sitting in the dugout. Someone was warming up on deck, swinging a black wooden bat. Mas placed his hands on his cheeks; he couldn't even say his name out loud or in his head. The first thing that came to him was Uno. Uno-*san*, the master outfielder—the first Japanese position player to be a major leaguer. Uno-*san* with the nobility of a samurai.

Mas and his all-American friend, Tug Yamada, who loved his Dodgers fourth after God, family, and friends, had both decided that Uno-*san* was quintessentially Japanese, in both his playing and his attitude. While his teammates hung out and laughed when others batted, Uno-*san* stayed in the zone. He stretched, he meditated, he focused. His work ethic was renowned. Uno-*san* was a private man who rarely gave interviews, but Tug's son, who also bled Dodger Blue, had discovered a perfect example of his dedication on an internet site. There he learned that Uno-*san* cleaned not only his mitt but also his cleats after each game *on his own*! This is a superstar earning several million dollars a year. To actually take care of his own soiled gear was unheard of.

Mas wished Tug was with him now, so they could both admire Uno-*san*'s form in person. Tug and his son, Joe, were coming later to the game, along with Haruo and his wife, Spoon, as well as their lawyer friend, G.I. Hasuike, and his girlfriend, Juanita. Mas's daughter, Mari, and grandson Takeo were also on their way. Since Genessee was at some kind of music conference, Mas was the only one who wasn't part of a pair. *Just like old times*, he thought. Sometimes flying solo was a relief, a gift. It made him feel that his life, at least for a moment, was wide open, not defined or boxed in by another person's expectations, desires, or disappointments.

The commotion near the opposing team's dugout was getting louder. The stadium apparently had limited cameramen and journalists to a narrow, rectangular space. Smitty looked like he was barking out instructions, but he was being ignored. The journalists continued to jostle for the best position to shoot the Japanese baseball *senshu* at practice. They were all Asian, except for one tall photographer, a Latino in a khaki vest who Mas had recognized as working for the local Japanese American newspaper in Los Angeles.

A thin *hakujin* girl with her blond hair in a ponytail emerged onto the field. She was pushing a cart of water bottles, and based on the muscle she was giving her load, it was a heavy one. Without giving it a thought, Mas took over the cart. His life was spent doing physical work—definitely second nature. He wheeled the cart next to Smitty.

"Thanks." The girl walked alongside him, wiping moisture from underneath her bangs.

"These guys are out of control. This is almost as bad as Nomomania," Smitty murmured to the girl, who was wearing the same Dodgers polo shirt.

"What?"

"You know, Hideo Nomo. The Japanese pitcher from the 1990s."

"Oh, yeah, there's a photo of him upstairs."

Smitty eyed Mas, giving him an exasperated shrug—*see*

what we old guys need to put up with? "Anyway, pass out the waters, April Sue," he told the girl. "The last thing we need is any of these journalists passing out from excitement."

April Sue dug her fingers in the plastic to uncase the water bottles. Even that seemed a struggle. Mas pulled out a small pocket knife, opened it, and cut into the packaging. "Thanks," the girl murmured again.

Mas grunted and helped her pass out waters to the members of the media.

"*Kuso*," one of them swore in Japanese to the photographer next to him. "Back off," he added, along with a sharp elbow jab. He then claimed the water bottle from Mas without even a token bow of the head.

Kuso, Mas silently repeated back to the journalist. This *kuso*-head wasn't holding onto a camera, but a notebook. He was dressed in a white linen suit and would have looked like a preacher if it wasn't for the shiny navy blue shirt and black leather tie. He was no youngster, unlike most of the ones holding onto poles with mounted cameras. Judging from the few gray hairs sprouting in his black goatee, Mas guessed the man to be at least forty.

"Shouldn't you be up there in the press box, Itai?" a cameraman in the back said.

Mas noticed that the speaker failed to tag the man's name with a "*san*," or Mister. No honorifics granted here, which meant he was probably viewed as pond scum.

"Get your cameras ready, everyone." Itai almost seemed to be bragging. "Because you'll soon witness the breaking of a story that will shake up the baseball world."

"Be quiet, no one wants to hear your shit." A sharp female voice cut through the male posturing. Instead of Japanese, she spoke an accented English. But it was perfectly understandable and heard. She was also dressed in a white suit, only instead of slacks, she wore a skirt. Her blouse was dotted with blue smears.

"What did you say?" Itai's voice took on the tone of a samurai declaring war.

"You heard me," she repeated in English. "We all know you're a slimy snake."

Itai pushed a few cameramen away as he approached the woman. "Some of us here are real journalists—"

"What's going on here?" The catcher who'd had such a hard time with Neko's knuckleball came forward. His mask was off his face, revealing dark eyes narrowed in a frown.

"It's nothing, Sawada-*kun*," the woman said to the catcher. "Right, Itt-*chan*?"

Itai looked sheepishly down at his feet and pushed his way back to his original position.

Mas was amazed. Itai was obviously intimidated by the catcher, this Sawada. But what amazed him even more were the honorifics the woman used: *kun* for Sawada, an intimate, affectionate term for males—close friends, family, and lovers—and *chan* for the jerk, Itai. *Chan* was usually for babies and children. Sawada's presence had reduced Itai to infantile status. And to further denigrate Itai, the woman snipped off the end of his name. This Sawada was someone to be be reckoned with, that was for sure.

Batting practice had apparently ended, because the entire

Japanese team was now making its way back to the dugout.

"Just because you're playing here, don't forget that I'm your *senpai*," the one with the bad blond dye job said to a thin, young player who looked only part Japanese.

"*Kohai, senpai*, that's old talk. Old Japan," said the young one. "This is the majors. The real thing."

The hairs on the back of Mas's neck stood on end. He remembered this kind of talk when he was in junior high school back in Hiroshima. The *senpai*, the elders, lorded over the younger ones, the *kohai*. Whatever the *senpai* ordered the *kohai* to do—whether it be lugging heavy rocks or cleaning the wooden floors of their classroom—the young ones had to obey. But the same rules apparently didn't apply on American soil.

"Maybe your head is getting too big for this stadium," said the blond player. "You haven't even made it out of the minors. And the way you've been pitching, who knows when that will happen."

The skinny man positioned himself right in front of his *senpai*. His long nose almost grazed his older teammate's pug one.

"*Yamare.*" Uno-*san* put an end to the squabbling between the two players. He apparently had enough stature on the team for both parties to listen. Yellow head went one way and the part-Japanese man went another.

Watching this exchange was another Asian woman who also stood on the sidelines. Mas had problems guessing any woman's age, but she looked to be around Mari's age or maybe a bit younger. She had an ID around her neck, but it didn't read "Press." Even though she wasn't in the press box, she kept taking photographs with her simple automatic camera. Mas briefly locked eyes with her and then quickly looked away.

Just then the Korean players began to take their places on the field. They wore white uniforms, and most of them were beefier looking than their Japanese counterparts. One carried a baseball, and Mas noticed that the fingernails on his right hand were immaculately polished. This must the knuckleballer for the Korean team. What was his name? Jin-Won Kim, Smitty had said.

Jin-Won's build was graceful—more like a dancer's. As Mas watched him approach the pitcher's mound, he wondered how he'd deal with the female knuckleballer, who was still up there. Would he elbow Neko off the mound like the journalists in the makeshift media box did? Would he give her the cold shoulder? Instead he spoke to her—Mas wondered if it was in English? Neko bowed, her face flushed pink. Jin-Won must have paid her some kind of compliment. Mas was shocked. First of all, they were competitors, members of opposing teams. And it went way beyond baseball; this was nation versus nation. And although it had been decades since Japan had colonized Korea, the resentment, especially among old-timers, remained deep. In fact, the early fans had already entered Dodger Stadium, with the Korean supporters waving Korean fans and hitting cowbells while the Japanese carried giant banners sporting their symbol, the singular red sun. Mas, on the field, could feel the heat of rivalry around him. National honor was at stake here.

That's even more of a reason why Mas couldn't understand Jin-Won's graciousness toward a Japanese player, especially a woman. Maybe there was some kind of special club that knuckleballers belonged to.

Mas knew he had to go back to where the lawnmowers were stored to do some maintenance work. But before he made his way back to left field, he knelt down to feel the grass. Soft as velvet, the individual blades were angled in different directions. For his son-in-law to be responsible for this carpet of grass was something that Mas could never have imagined.

Mas took in a few more breaths from the field and then heard a loud commotion coming from the Japanese journalists again. Only this wasn't a fight for the best position. Itai was on the ground, and most of the cameramen were aiming their lenses on him instead of helping. His chest was pumping fast—up and down, up and down. He then vomited and the photographer, the one from the L.A. newspaper, turned Itai over on his side. "Call 911," he yelled, but Smitty was already on it.

Mas watched the goateed man's face turn tomato red, and then his body became completely still. The entire press corps, which seconds earlier had been eager to document Itai's struggle with life, lowered their cameras and notebooks. It was clear to all, even Mas. Death had won.

Chapter Two

The next hour was a blur. The LAPD had descended in a matter of minutes as officers had already been patrolling the parking lot. Two men appeared with a metal gurney; they put Itai's body on it and covered it with a dark cloth that read "L.A. Coroner."

"Are they going to cancel the game?" Mas overhead April Sue ask Smitty as the gurney was quickly wheeled out of view.

"We have a game to play with TV crews from fifteen countries. A dead journalist from Japan isn't going to stop anything."

Most of the police officers also dispersed, leaving only two male investigators—one black and one white—wearing dress shirts and ties. The press was being escorted from the field into the stadium. Based on the humming *monku* of the Japanese journalists, their removal was under protest.

Mas put his head down and attempted to make his way back to the equipment storage area. He had barely taken two steps when he heard a harsh male voice, the sound of twisted rusty metal.

"Wait a minute. You. We need a few words with you."

Mas turned to see one of the men in suits—the *hakujin* man, his brown, wavy hair whipped to one side like dead branches on the side of a highway. Lloyd—where did he come from?—appeared suddenly, standing in front of Mas, a human shield. "That's my father-in-law. He had nothing to do with any of this. He's just here to sharpen some lawn-mower blades—"

"We need to question everyone on the field, and that includes him." The detective studied Mas. "What, he can't speak English?"

"I can speak orai."

The detective hesitated, as if he didn't quite understand. "It'll just be a few minutes."

Lloyd relented. After all, the boy had responsibilities. This was his first big event since the promotion, and the hub-bub of the dead journalist had delayed his final field prep.

As it turned out, it wasn't just a few minutes. It was forty-nine to be exact. Mas knew because about every five minutes he checked his digital Casio watch, held together only with twine around his wrist. He and the journalists had to sit in the hallway inside the stadium as one person at a time was called into a room named after one of the Dodger's former managers, Tommy Lasorda. It was worse than a doctor's waiting room.

Finally, the detective with the wind-blown hair, the one who'd spoken to him, appeared. "You," he gestured toward Mas. "You're next."

Mas grimaced. He'd had encounters with homicide detectives before, and only half of them had been good. He had a feeling this one would not fall in that category.

Already sitting at a table in the room was the black detective. He was young and clean shaven, wearing a colorful tie with rainbow swirls. He introduced himself as Detective Cortez Williams and extended his hand for Mas to shake. Mas took it—what alternative did he have? Williams looked like he was eighteen years old. Mas wondered if the LAPD was that desperate these days. The ugly one, Detective Garibay, sat beside him, studying the dirt under his nails.

"What's your full name?" Williams asked.

"Mas—Masao Arai."

He had to repeat the spelling a couple of times before the detective got it.

"So tell me about yourself, Mr. Arai."

"I'zu gardener. Gotsu son-in-law who's now in charge of the field. Heezu one brought me on board."

"Did you know Mr. Itai from before?"

"Neva seen his face. Neva heard of him." Mas's life would certainly have been better if that remained the case. "Just helpin' dat girlu." Mas silently cursed the skinny blonde, April Sue. Why hadn't he just held back from helping her? Ten years ago he would have. But lately Mas found himself getting involved in things that he never would have in the past.

"So did someone hand you that water to give to Mr. Itai?"

The water. So that's what they were after. Did it have

something to do with Itai's death?

"I just grab and give it ova to him."

Detective Williams scribbled something in his notebook.

"Did you take it from April Sue or someone else? Or did you pull it from the rest of the bottles?"

Mas explained that it had been randomly pulled. It could have been any of the bottles with the Dodgers label.

"Mr. Arai, would it be okay if we took your fingerprints? Just so we can exclude them."

★   ★   ★

"I gotsu fingerprinted," Mas announced after leaving the Tommy Lasorda room.

His daughter, Mari, was there in the open walkway, as well as his grandson, Takeo, and Lloyd.

"What the hell, Lloyd? How could you let that happen?" Mari said.

Takeo grabbed hold of Mas's right palm and examined it closely. "Are you getting arrested, Grandpa?"

"It's just routine," Lloyd interrupted. His ridiculous sunglasses were now perched on his head. "That guy probably just had a heart attack. It wouldn't have been a big deal if someone hadn't said that he'd probably been killed. And then someone from the coroner's office confirmed that the body looked suspicious."

Outside they heard the cheers of the crowd.

"You can still see most of the game," Lloyd said to Mas. "It's not like you missed much of anything."

Mari then assumed a very familiar position—all five feet of her erect, hands on her hips, staring up at her six-footer husband. "Are you kidding me? A man just died, Lloyd. Right on the field. My father just witnessed it, and you want us to pretend everything is fine?"

"I'zu orai." And really, Mas was all right, or at least he thought he was. He had, unfortunately, witnessed much, much worse. "No good leavin' those other guys all by themselves." Lloyd had secured group seats for not only the family, but all of their friends.

"Well, you come, too," Mari said. "There's a seat for you."

"Gonna just take it easy for a while."

"It's not like you can drive yourself home. You came with Lloyd, remember?"

"Meetcha by the store when game ova?" Mas asked. That was their regular meeting spot.

Mari gave her husband a parting frown. "See, I told you it was too much."

Mas didn't bother to say goodbye. He didn't like a big to-do. When he decided something, it was decided. And he decided that he needed to be by himself.

He wandered and checked out the displays in the stadium's hallways, where the big shots roamed. In the corner was a little bug of a vehicle, painted like a baseball, which they once used to bring in the relief pitchers. Other funny memorabilia were displayed on the walls. Farther down the hall were rows of shiny trophies, gold catchers' mitts, and engraved trophies.

Even though Mas wore a lanyard with a laminated pass, no one checked to see if he was official. They probably figured that he was a janitor. Someone harmless. Utterly forgettable.

In one of the side display rooms, he encountered another person. An Asian woman about his age. She stood in front of a row of baseball bats engraved with names of former Dodgers. She wore a jacket with "Korea" stitched in the back, so it was clear who she was rooting for.

Mas dipped his head. "Hallo." *What the hell.* He had to say something.

"*Konnichiwa*," she responded in Japanese.

Was it that obvious that his roots were back in Japan? It wasn't unusual for people straight from Korea to start talking to him in Japanese, but it made him uncomfortable, like he was suddenly in a position to be the colonizer. As soon as he could, he excused himself and headed in the opposite direction.

Outside he heard the roaring of the crowds, the clanking of the bells, the hum of the organ. To hear such excitement made him feel melancholy for a moment—he was again outside of the circle, the pulse of the heart.

He thought of Genessee for a moment—the gap between her front teeth, her dark and animated eyes. She could talk with her eyes, he thought. That's one thing that he appreciated about her. That they could be dead silent yet Mas would know what she was thinking.

Was it love? He wasn't quite sure what love was. He met Chizuko just weeks before they were to get married. She, like Genessee, was a brain, big on reading and investigating details. With Chizuko, it was everyday things like tax rebates and the best college for Mari, while with Genessee it was beyond their homes and mundane lives: the world and music.

Had Mas loved Chizuko? That was almost an insulting question. They'd been beyond love. They didn't need red roses or silly Hallmark cards to prove their commitment to anyone. But Mas hadn't been constantly at Chizuko's side during her chemo treatments—and he still felt badly for that. It wasn't that he didn't love her; it was that he cared for her too much. To see this vibrant woman wasting away and getting sick to her stomach was too much for Mas. He knew now that he was capable of doing more. But it was too late. It almost had been too late to mend his relationship with Mari, but he'd answered the call. And now the four of them were squeezed in his two-bedroom in Altadena.

Genessee never mentioned anything about love, thank goodness. But her eyes said love. Mas could see it as she looked over from her couch and gazed at Mas while he watched an old Western on TV. It caught him by surprise. Why would this part-time professor want to spend so much time with him, a semi-retired gardener? He was, however, grateful for her desire.

Mas took the elevator to the top of the stadium and walked by murals heralding the stadium's past. Long lines for Dodger dogs and beer stretched out from concession stands—a tangle of stout, tall men of all colors, women in blue and red T-shirts, crying babies wetting their jumpers.

For a moment, Mas felt like he couldn't breathe. Even though they were all out in the open air, it seemed like the air was heavy, pressing down. He needed an escape from all the people. He needed quiet. He needed green.

Mas walked through the exit and past the sculptures of giant numbers, all belonging to the Dodger greats, all retired. Number 42, Jackie Robinson, back in Brooklyn, before the move to Chavez Ravine. Number 39, Roy Campanella, the catcher for the Brooklyn Dodgers. Number 32, Sandy Koufax, the southpaw pitcher. In the hush of emptiness here, were their spirits present?

Seeing that man die in front of him, the *kuso*-head Itai, had indeed taken a toll on Mas. Mari knew him better than he would like to admit. One moment, Itai had been bellowing and bragging, and another moment, struggling for air. Mas had seen something like that before, but it was decades earlier, buried and unimaginable.

One of the first times he stayed over at Genessee's, his yelling during his sleep had frightened her.

"You were crying 'help!' " she said, her eyes shiny with tears. " 'Give us water!' "

Mas dismissed it as indigestion. "Shoulda neva eat chili and onions." But in his heart of hearts, he knew what it was about. Chizuko had also spoken about his late-night cries. He decided then that he shouldn't sleep over at Genessee's anymore.

It was a bit indecent anyway, especially when Genessee went to church the next Sunday morning. Marriage would make everything decent, but then what would Mas lose? His freedom, for one, but even more was his identity, and perhaps his late wife's identity. If he went and got married, he'd no longer be seen as a widower. And if he wasn't a widower anymore, would Chizuko's existence be somehow erased?

He walked faster down the curve of the driveway into the sinkhole of the parking lot. Outside the stadium, which glowed with fluorescent lights, he felt even more alone. If he didn't belong inside with his family, where did he belong?

And then he remembered. The Japanese garden. What was it that Smitty had said? That the garden could be found along a line from home base to second. Formerly parking lot 37, close to where a Union 76 station had once pumped gas. Mas walked in between the parked cars to make his way to a hill shaded by ill-shapen pine and cedar trees.

When he finally reached the edge, he came face to face with a tall, black iron fence with a sign that was menacing in its simplicity: "No Trespassing." The gate, which was too high for him to scale, had a simple lock that was probably easy to pick. But he didn't have to go to such lengths, because with one jiggle, the gate opened.

Did Mas even dare? He looked back at the lit stadium, the vortex of life. Was someone watching him as he made his way down here? Were there secret cameras mounted on those light poles? But he saw nothing. No police, no guards. Everything was focused on the game and the spectators. Not out here in a dirty corner of the parking lot.

Mas quickly went through the gate and closed it behind him. No sense attracting attention. There was still some light left, so he was able to see the broken cement stairs that took him up the dried-out hill. Did they ever bother to water this area?

When he finally reached the top, Mas felt weak in the knees. It wasn't the climb that did it. It was what he saw. Dead, uprooted pine trees. Stones thrown haphazardly like giant dice. Dead grass. If a garden could bleed, this one would be covered in blood.

A *toro*, a Japanese stone lantern, was the only evidence that something artful had once lived here. It was large, maybe ten feet tall. These things were not cheap; Mas knew because he'd acquired smaller versions for the "Oriental" gardens some of his customers had requested in the past. With the fallen trees beside it, the *toro* seemed like a lone survivor in a war zone.

Sabishii. Mas felt the loneliness creep into his bones. Who had ravaged—or perhaps, more appropriately, ignored—this Japanese garden? He stumbled around the bleak area one more time while the sky quickly lost light. He discovered a cement monument base in a corner and could barely make out the letters on its plaque. Something about the hundred-year anniversary of immigration from Korea. Did the Koreans even know that such a recognition was here?

Mas then heard the crunch of dead branches up the hill. It wasn't surprising that creatures invaded this place when the sun went down. And when he saw headlights flash on the cars in the distance, Mas knew his exit was overdue.

★ ★ ★

"Grandpa, you should have seen it! Japan won with a sa-yonara slam!" Takeo, his right hand encased in a blue foam mitt with a giant raised index finger, ran up to Mas.

"Sayonara *nani*?" Mas was breathing hard after his illegal trespass of the Japanese garden. He'd barely made it on time to their meeting place.

"That's a grand slam. That's what Uncle Tug calls it," Takeo explained.

Sure enough, the large and sturdy body of Tug Yamada followed behind Takeo. A slap on Mas's back. "Hey, old man. We heard about the incident. You okay?"

Mas nodded. Just hearing the baritone voice of his most stable friend made his stomach churn. Just from Tug asking, Mas realized that he wasn't that okay. "Orai, orai," he lied. Desperate to change the subject, he gestured toward the overgrown thatch of diseased trees. "You knowsu there a Japanese garden ova there?"

"What? A Japanese garden? I don't think so."

"He's right, Dad," responded Joe, a font of sports trivia. "It was built in the sixties. I think a Japanese sportswriter gave some kind of stone lantern or something to Walter O'Malley and the Dodgers."

"Never heard of such a thing," said Tug. "Why don't they show it off or something?"

Mas moved with the group and the rest of the crowd. "Nuttin' to show off. Saw it with my own eyes. Evertin' dead."

"You don't say." Tug slowed his pace. "They let you in there?"

"Where were you, Dad?" Why did Mari always pop out of nowhere?

"No place."

"Our car is over in Lot L. We'll see you guys later," Mari said to Tug and Joe.

As they began to separate in their different directions, Tug called out to Mas. "So you're going to come over to my place tomorrow, right? Lil says I need to fix the washer pronto. Haruo said he's coming, too."

Mas lifted his hand in acknowledgment. Ah, *shikata-ganai*. He couldn't refuse. With only one customer these days, it's not like he could say he was working.

"So what were you saying? Something about a Japanese garden?" Mari, like their old dog, could never let anything go.

"Just that I heard one is out there. Back in parkin' lot." Mas got an idea. "Maybe you can make a movie about it or sumptin?"

"I don't think a Japanese garden at Dodger Stadium will really interest anyone, Dad. These days it's all about platform and crowdfunding. Remember when I tried to pitch a project about Japanese Peruvians based on Juanita's parents' experience? How they were taken from Peru and locked up in Texas to be part of a prisoner exchange program? If I can't get that off the ground, who'll want to fund a documentary on an old garden in a baseball stadium?"

Mas didn't catch everything that his daughter said, but he got the general message. Gardens, not to mention gardeners, were definitely out of fashion.

As Takeo usually liked to ride shotgun with his mother, Mas was only too happy to ride alone in the back seat. They sat for some time in the darkness, frozen in place by the never-ending line of cars waiting for release from the stadium. Mari put on some music, a woman singing along with a simple tune played on a piano. Mas wasn't much of a music person, but he preferred this to talking. Soon they heard the short breaths of Takeo sleeping, and finally the car jerked forward as the logjam cleared. As they flowed through the stadium's gates, Mas silently said goodbye to the lone *toro*.

★ ★ ★

Takeo was too heavy to carry anymore, so Mari jostled him awake and led him through the house to the back room connected to the kitchen.

Mas, on the other hand, headed straight for the kitchen. He was famished, since he didn't have a chance to eat a Dodger dog because of the Itai incident. He found a fistful of rice in Mari's high-tech cooker that used something called fuzzy logic. Squirts of hot water from an electric carafe into a porcelain teapot holding day-old tea leaves. A crunchy red pickled plum from a bottle in the refrigerator. Put all that in a Japanese bowl and stir with the ends of chopsticks.

As he was slurping down his *ochazuke* in the blessed silence of the kitchen, the back door opened. *Well, that didn't last long*, he thought. And while Lloyd usually headed to the bathroom to take a shower after work, he instead—unfortunately for Mas—took a seat at the kitchen table.

"What a mess," he said, taking off his cap, the sunglasses still propped on top of it. "Those reporters are maniacs. They make the paparazzi here seem like lap dogs."

Mas got up with his empty bowl and rinsed it in the sink. He wasn't in the mood to hear about his son-in-law's long day. He went to the living room and clicked the remote for the television set, which was tuned to Japanese programming. Sinking into his easy chair, he was again none too happy to see Lloyd getting comfortable in the chair next to him.

"Hey," Lloyd pointed to the screen. "It's that reporter at the game."

The woman was wearing the same blue dotted blouse. Her hair was cleaned up and her lipstick more red than Mas remembered.

Mas listened for a moment. The reporter introduced herself as Amika Hadashi. In her rhythmic Japanese, she described how the Japanese team had beaten Korea and how Uno-*san* had hit the winning grand slam in the ninth inning.

"Nuttin' about the dead man. Itai," he reported to his son-in-law.

"You know his name?"

Itai was easy to remember. Although the name's *kanji* was probably written differently in Japanese, *itai* usually meant pain. And judging from his colleagues' reaction to him, Itai was indeed the biggest pain around.

"She looks pretty sweet on TV, but she's quite another thing in person," said Lloyd. "I saw her during the game in the hallway outside the Tommy Lasorda room. I think it was when you were being interviewed. She was totally laying into April Sue, saying that she was incompetent. She made the girl cry."

Mas bit down on his dentures. He wasn't a fan of the skinny blonde, but she didn't deserve being yelled at in public.

"And after the game, she was on the field for a long time doing her interviews. I wanted to turn off the lights, but she kept talking to one of the players for what seemed like an hour."

"Catcha, huh?"

"No, actually, that was the strange thing. It was with one of the Korean players. The knuckleball pitcher."

What? That didn't make sense. Why would a Japanese reporter want to spend so much time with a player from the losing team?

"Everyone in bed?" Lloyd asked, taking his cap off and rubbing his shaved head.

Mas nodded, and then announced, "I see dat Japanese garden."

"What Japanese garden?"

"One ova in parkin' lot."

"Oh, yeah, I heard something about that."

Mas was mystified. At one time, Lloyd would have been all over anything Japanese, especially a garden. Now he was obsessed with grass, fertilizing turf, and drawing perfectly straight lines in chalk.

"You change," Mas declared.

"What do you mean, I've changed?"

Mas dragged himself out of his chair. He didn't need to repeat himself. He knew what he saw. *Uragirimono*. A turncoat who hid his true colors inside. Yes, Mas's only son-in-law had officially become a sellout.

Chapter Three

I didn't wake you, did I?" It was Genessee's voice, warm and cozy, in his ear.

Mas straightened the telephone receiver. "No," he lied. He wasn't sure what time it was, but based on the dim light hitting his crooked blinds, it must not yet be six o'clock in the morning.

"How was the baseball game?"

Mas could have told Genessee all about Itai, but there was no reason to worry her.

"Orai," Mas said.

"Just checking if you can still pick me up tonight. I know it's late. I can ask my son—"

"No, I come, no trouble," Mas lied again.

Even with the Steve McQueen glasses, Mas's eyes weren't what they used to be. Going to LAX in the middle of the night wasn't his idea of a good time. But at least it should be late enough for traffic to have eased and maybe early enough for the drunkards to still be inside drinking.

"Howsu convention?"

"It's amazing. Some professors are here from Okinawa, and they brought musical instruments—some of them are a hundred years old." As Genessee prattled on, energized by her adventures, Mas couldn't help but let his mind wander. The terrible death of Itai hadn't been a dream. Did the police have more information on the cause of his demise?

"So what are your plans for today?" That was Genessee's favorite question. She was into planning because she was fully in charge of her life, while Mas instead often let life happen to him. But he did have one plan.

"Helping Tug fix his washer. Haruo comin' along, too."

"Well, you know, there are professionals for those things."

Mas chose to ignore her comment. To call any of them amateurs was beyond insulting.

"Gotsu go. Bye-bye."

"Bye, Mas." Genessee hesitated, and he worried that she'd add something to her farewell. Before she could, he hung up.

★ ★ ★

"Missed you last night, Mas," Haruo said as Mas walked through Tug's open garage. As he aged, Haruo's scar on the left side of his face seemed to lose its elasticity. It lay on his face like something foreign, like the surface of a rubber chicken.

Haruo had been a repeat married man for some time now. More than five years. This was his second go-round, and this union seemed to suit him. While his ex-wife, Yasuko, was sharp edged, Spoon was, both physically and emotionally, softer. The two wives were both Japanese, but Yasuko was born in Japan, while Spoon was a Nisei who had spent her teen years in camp during World War II. She had low expectations of America and apparently of family as well. Certainly good ingredients for a successful marriage with Haruo.

"Youzu have a good time?" Mas asked, which he knew was a ridiculous question the minute he said it. With Haruo, life was always good, even if he was mere steps from calamity.

"Grand slam, Mas! Too bad you miss it. Hey, the ball almost go outta the park."

"I've only seen seven of those in my whole life," Tug added. "It was a beautiful thing." Tug and his son were the types to bring blank scorecards and record the stats of who pitched, who hit, and who made errors.

"Sorry to hear about dead guy," Haruo said. "Youzu hear anytin' new?"

Mas shook his head, not making eye contact. Haruo instantly understood that the conversation was closed.

They worked silently, methodically.

Mas had the best hands for the job. Tug's were too meaty—plus, he was missing part of his forefinger. Haruo had only one good eye, and that eye wasn't even so good anymore. Luckily Tug's washer was at least ten years old and basic—no fancy electronic equipment to dismantle. Just a lot of tiny screws, which Tug was in charge of keeping track of, which he did with snack-size plastic bags and Post-Its.

Finally, with the turn of a nut screw, they were able to get the washer bucket loose and clean out the strings of fabric that had gotten caught in it.

About two hours into their work, Lil came out with a tray of cold barley tea and homemade cookies. She'd had hip replacement surgery a few years back and now apparently had a new lease on life. Even her face, despite the lines around the eyes and neck, seemed younger and more alert.

"You all deserve a break," she said, setting the tray down on an old metal trunk—maybe even Tug's old footlocker from fighting in Europe in World War II. "I told Tug that we could call the handyman, but he insisted in doing it himself. Which, of course, included you two."

They didn't waste any time in glugging down the tea but practiced more restraint when it came to the cookies.

"How's Genessee? Haven't seen her in a while." Lil, who was obviously delighted that Mas had a "lady friend," always kept tabs to see if she was still in the picture.

"Sheezu in San Francisco. For a conference with other *erai* people," Haruo piped up. *Erai* meant smart, which obviously didn't include Mas.

"Comin' home tonight." Mas finished the last sip of tea and finally grabbed a cookie after Tug helped himself to one. "Sah, back to work?"

They silently resumed their positions. They secured the washer tub and put the whole basket back into its frame. They were on their fifth screw when Haruo reluctantly excused himself. His wife, Spoon, had retired their flower business, but Dee had started a wholesale business in Hawaiian tropical flowers, specializing in leis for special occasions like graduations and anniversaries. There was a golden anniversary that night, and Haruo had agreed to do the delivery to El Monte.

That left Mas alone with Tug, which was just as well. Tug didn't talk as much as Haruo, which made the reassembly go faster. After they'd fastened the last screw, Mas sat back in one of the Yamadas' lawn chairs while Tug wiped the sweat off of his forehead with an old towel.

"We may be going to Toronto next week," Tug announced. "Or we may not."

Mas looked up, curious. Usually the Yamadas planned their international trips months in advance.

Tug's voice became thin and deliberate. "You see, Joy's getting married."

"Toronto, thatsu Canada, *desho*? Who wiz?" Last Mas heard, Joy had a lady friend of her own, a Latina whose roots were in Puerto Rico. Her name was a flower, Mas thought he remembered.

"Iris. Didn't you meet her last Christmas?"

Mas nodded. He didn't know what to say. He knew that Tug and Lil were stalwart members of Sunrise Baptist Church in Little Tokyo. He had no idea about the church's position on same-sex marriage, but he figured it wasn't too open.

"Thatsu good," Mas said, more in the tone of a question than a statement. "*Omedetou*," he offered his congratulations in Japanese.

"Lil's not taking it well, as you can imagine. I guess she

dreamed that her little girl would be going down the aisle in a white dress, even though that little girl is now in her mid-forties."

"No white dress in those kinds of weddings?"

"No, it's not that. I'm not even sure what they'll be wearing. But I guess Lil also thought the groom would be a nice young man in a tuxedo, not a woman with a snake tattoo on her arm."

Mas nodded. Yes, he remembered the tattoo now. He spotted it when she was sitting at the Yamadas' dinner table, Iris's arm loosely dangling from the back of Joy's chair. Life, especially when it came to children, was full of surprises. If you told Mas back in 1999 that his daughter and her family would be living with him in ten years, he'd have laughed in your face.

But this was not a laughing matter for Tug. There were his faith and family to consider. This wedding, Mas assumed, was putting both to the test.

"Lil feels that if we attend, we approve. But if we don't go, I don't think Joy will ever talk to us again."

Mas didn't know what to say. Even though he had Mari, he was no expert on father-daughter relationships, except maybe on the things you should avoid. And as for religion, that wasn't something he was familiar with, although he did occasionally accompany Genessee to church—ironically, sometimes after his sleepovers. The last time, the minister talked about judging other people, how you shouldn't do it. Something about needing to take a three-by-five out of your eye. Such talk mystified Mas. How could you even put something that large in your eye in the first place?

"Sumptin about love. You Christians talk a lot about it. And forgive, too."

It was now time for Tug to chuckle. "Yes, two of the biggest proponents of our religion." His face then became more serious. "But it's hard to know how to love. It's not easy."

That Mas could agree with. And that was why he didn't like how the *hakujin* threw around the "love" word so much. They *loved* this movie, they *loved* this car, they *loved* this flower. The word had become so weak that it failed to spark any real emotion.

The conversation had taken such a serious tone that Mas scrambled to find something else to talk about. He spied the program from last night's baseball game on Tug's work bench and flipped to the dog-eared page with photos of all the players.

Mas hadn't seen the program, and it fascinated him to see the head shots of the players. The yellow-haired one was named Kii Tanji, and he played for the Yomiuri Giants in Tokyo. The young *hapa* pitcher was Soji Zahed—what kind of name was Zahed? Sounded Arabian to Mas. The catcher, Sawada, was with the Colorado Rockies, but Mas wasn't that familiar with him.

Tug pointed at yellow head, Tanji. "This one was actually very impressive," he said. "He's the second baseman. A journeyman player. I think he's in his late thirties. Helped make a double play. Got a man out at second and then threw the ball perfectly to home."

"But not good enough for majors." Mas remembered

Tanji's altercation with the pitcher, Zahed.

"I guess it's all about timing."

Mas agreed. Just like Uno-*san*—the stars had aligned regarding the timing of his free agency, which made it possible to come to America. He mentioned that to Tug, who nodded. "He was spectacular yesterday, wasn't he? Oh, you missed his home run."

"But I see him on the field. Maybe two feet away."

"You did? Did you talk to him?" Before Mas could respond, Tug withdrew his question. "No, of course not. He probably was in the zone."

Mas rose to his feet. It was late, almost dinnertime. The washer was restored, and there was no reason to stay any longer.

★ ★ ★

When Mas pulled the Impala into the driveway, Mari, much like she did when she was a child, was looking at him through the screen door. She pushed it open as he walked up, and the words rushed out. "I'm glad you're here. We've been calling you on your cell, Dad. You should carry it with you."

Mas frowned. What was this all about? "I carry," he said, digging it out from the corner of his pocket.

Mari flipped it open. "But it needs to be *on*. Never mind that right now. You have a visitor. From Hiroshima."

The first people who came to mind were his siblings, at least the couple that were still alive. And then—no, it couldn't be. Akemi? Mas blushed in embarrassment for what he was thinking. He wasn't a married man, but he was the next closest thing to it.

Mari had to almost push him into the living room. Mas's eyes, through his glasses, had to adjust to the light. Instead of an old Japanese woman sitting on his couch, there was a young Japanese man, also wearing glasses, but his were thick black-rimmed ones.

Mas had no idea who this person was. The man quickly got to his feet and began to speak in Japanese. "Arai-*san*, it's me, Kimura Yukikazu. Yuki. I'm Akemi's grandson. My magazine sent me here to replace Itai-*san*."

"He said he knows you, Dad." Mari came to Mas's side. "That he even stayed here before, ten years ago."

Yuki nodded. "Yes, yes," he said in halting English. "My grandmother and I sleep here. Then the police come and arrest me."

"What?!"

Takeo, his head wet presumingly from a bath, entered the living room. "Who's that, Mom?"

"That's what I'm trying to figure out."

Mas noticed a backpack next to the couch. Oh no, he wasn't thinking of staying here, was he?

"Dis my daughta, Mari," Mas kept speaking in English for all to understand. "Grandson, Takeo."

Yuki gestured with his right hand toward Mari. "You the one never call. No contact with Mista Arai back then, ten years ago?"

Mari's mouth fell open. "Dad, who is this guy?"

"Sorry, my name Yukikazu Kimura," he repeated. "Or

Yuki. Reporter with *Nippon Series*." He fished out a business card from the inside of his blazer and presented it to Mari with two hands, as was customary.

"I don't have a card. I didn't think it was necessary…in my own house."

Chotto matte, Mas thought. *This is* my *house*. But that technicality aside, he was faced with a more pressing matter. "I thought you work for *Shine*."

Yuki switched over to Japanese. "Oh, that went out of business after a couple of years. *Nippon Series* is a respectable publication. It's been around for twenty-five years."

Oh, yah, a lifetime, Mas thought. *Maybe your lifetime.* He took the conversation back to English. "Whatchu doin' here? Youzu probably want to stay in Little Tokyo. I can take you ova." *Right before I pick up Genessee from the airport.*

"I have job for Arai-*san*."

"A job?" Mari's fists were on her hips.

"I need driver. And translator."

"You realize that my father is almost eighty years old, right? And his English skills aren't the best."

"I need man I can trust," Yuki said emphatically. "I read and understand much English, but speaking, not so good."

Somehow those words softened both Mas and Mari. *What a magician Yuki had become*, Mas thought.

"How much?" Mas asked.

"No, Dad—"

"How much do you charge?" Yuki threw that question back to Mas in Japanese.

"Hundred a day." That's how much he charged during

the heyday of his gardening route. The coins and bills in the Yuban coffee can in his closet were getting low due to the new residents at the house.

"Hundred. Okay. I'zu here a week."

Mas extended his hand. "Orai. Deal."

"I don't know about this—" Mari was still skeptical.

"Dis my life. My bizness."

★ ★ ★

Mas directed the boy out the door and into the driveway, where his Impala was parked. Mari moved her hybrid Honda out of the way, while Takeo, barefoot and hair still damp, waited on the porch.

"Hey, what happened to your truck? Finally broke down?" Yuki spoke in Japanese as he put his backpack in the trunk. "Actually, this car is pretty old, too."

Mas didn't like to tell the story of how he'd lost the truck, so he did what he usually did. Ignored the question.

Before they left the driveway, Mari flagged down Mas, causing him to roll down the window. "What time will you be home?"

"Late." She didn't need to know about his midnight drive to the airport. In that way, she was like her mother. Always weighed down by *shinpai*. Worry, Mas found, was like cockroaches. Worries only led to more worries.

Yuki said he was registered at one of the hotels in Little Tokyo. Mas was familiar with it. The boy had come a long way from what he had been.

"So you're a real reporter," Mas said in Japanese.

"Yes, a real one. You seem surprised."

"You know I was there. When that Itai died on the field."

Yuki squirmed in his seat. Mas knew this was no coincidence. "I saw your photo in some of the digital prints our freelancer sent us," he finally admitted. "Akemi had mentioned that you had a son-in-law who works for the Dodgers."

Mas changed back to English. It seemed safer that way. He needed some kind of barrier to separate himself from the reporter. "So youzu don't need me to drive youzu around."

"No, I do need you," said Yuki, staying in Japanese. "I never got my license in Japan. I work now in Tokyo. I need a person I can depend on, who knows his way around Los Angeles."

Mas frowned. *What was the big deal?* "Dis baseball story, *desho*? How come such mystery?"

"You don't know, do you?" Yuki said. "I'm not here for the World Championship. I'm here to investigate what happened to Itai-*san*. He didn't die from natural causes, Arai-*san*. I mean, he had high blood pressure, but he took medicine for that."

Mas almost lost control of the steering wheel.

"He's always received death threats. He was that kind of journalist. I guess this time someone made good on it."

"How about you?"

Yuki was quiet. "Had my share, too."

Mas shivered. Here he was, the driver for a man who might be targeted. He'd already been in a car accident that had threatened his life. He didn't need to be in another one.

"By the way, Akemi says hello," Yuki said.

"Oh, yah."

"She's still single. All by herself in Hiroshima."

"Sure she likesu dat way."

"I'm not so sure."

Mas didn't know why he was feeling guilty. There was absolutely nothing between him and Akemi. And if there was, that was before World War II, when he was just a boy.

"So see you tomorrow? You can come up to my room. I'm in 302."

Mas had to admit that a part of him appreciated being needed. When did anyone say that he or she needed Mas Arai, and only Mas?

Of course, Yuki was not the only person who needed him today. Mas got on the 110 and took a straight shot to the 105, a newborn-baby freeway in comparison. The 105 took him directly to LAX and at that time of night, the drive was thankfully fast.

He'd made sure to turn on his clamshell phone this time, and it chirped cheerfully—a sign that Genessee had indeed arrived. And there she was on the curb, the familiar silhouette of her thin frame and the halo of her short-cropped Afro.

She pushed her suitcase in the back before settling in the passenger seat. "Thanks for picking me up," she said. "So, did anything happen while I was away?"

Chapter Four

L uckily, Genessee was dead tired, so when Mas answered her invitation to come into her house with a blank stare, she didn't seem bothered.

"I have a long day tomorrow, anyway," she said, adding that she was supposed to babysit her grandchildren the next morning.

She gave him a peck on the cheek while Mas patted her back a couple of times. Physical affection in public, even under the cover of night and on the quiet front porch, was uncomfortable for him.

As he returned to the Impala, he felt bad that he hadn't mentioned anything about his new "job." But how to explain his relationship with Yuki Kimura? Genessee was like Chizuko in that she enjoyed digging for details. Inevitably Akemi's name would come up, and how to describe their childhood friendship? Would she sense in a catch in his throat that something had happened between them in the past? It was only a kiss between teenagers, but it had been his first. And one that had never been forgotten.

The next day he was again awakened by a phone call. It was even before the noise of the Jensen family, so he knew it was early.

"Let's go, *Ojisan*." To hear the familiar term "uncle" once again caught Mas off guard. He had surprisingly missed it.

"Wheresu we goin'?"

"Goin' to where Itai-*san* was staying."

"Where?"

"Relative's house. Sunny Hirose. In Soteru."

Sawtelle. Mas frowned. That was practically where UCLA was located, on the other side of town. Another long drive. *Think of the money*, he reminded himself. One hundred dollars.

"Right now?" He brought his Casio watch to his nose. It was six o'clock in the morning. No time to be knocking on people's doors.

"Around ten o'clock. I'll have a US cell phone by then. And then a press conference at Dodger Stadium."

When Mas arrived at Yuki's hotel, the boy was waiting at the curb with a piece of clothing in his hands.

"Can you wear this polo shirt?" Yuki said after he was in the passenger seat and they'd exchanged niceties. "You'd look more professional."

Sonofagun. First Lloyd gets all high-tone with his expensive sunglasses and expensive haircut. (Mas had volunteered to mow down his hair with an electric shaver for free, but for some reason Lloyd declined.) And now this from the Japanese boy wonder.

When they reached a traffic light, Mas pulled the polo shirt over his T-shirt. The logo for *Nippon Series*—a large

N and S—was stitched on the front left of the shirt. The light changed to green; with the polo shirt still scrunched up above his belly, Mas stepped on the gas pedal. Yuki was fixated on his cell phone, as all people, including his own family members, seemed to be these days. It's a wonder that they even know what each other looks like. Their gazes always down on the screen, not on faces.

Yuki tapped on his screen, unleashing a robotic female voice telling him to make a left turn on Olive Street.

"I knowsu how to get to Soteru." Mas frowned. "Once we getsu closer you can let the phone talk."

As he went from the 110 to the 10, Mas wondered what they would say to the relative. Wouldn't this be the ultimate *jama*, or bother, to barge into a stranger's house after a loved one was murdered? The police—maybe even the detectives who'd questioned Mas back at Dodger Stadium—probably had been there. *I just drive, I just drive*, Mas told himself. Maybe he could just stay in the Impala if Yuki didn't need translation assistance.

As Mas guided the car from one lane to another, he gradually began to feel better. The LAPD would find out who killed the Japanese journalist. Yuki didn't have the know-how to tackle something like this.

"Get off where?" Mas finally asked when he went north on the 405.

"So you're allowing my phone to speak now?" Yuki gave a slip of a smile and tapped on his phone again. "Let's see what Akemi tells us."

"Akemi?"

"That's what I decided to call my phone. So my grand-mother is still close to me."

Mas grimaced. He had heard of mama's boys, but a grandma's boy? That was carrying it too far.

"You can talk to her anytime," Yuki said. "My real grandmother, I mean. I'm going to have her number pro-grammed in here. You can Skype her and it won't cost me hardly anything."

Mas didn't know why Yuki was pushing Akemi so hard on him. He couldn't say that he didn't want to talk to her. But the past was finally the past. Mas was advancing for-ward, but just when he thought he was totally free of the past, something would grab hold of his foot and not let go.

The house was a neat, white ranch-style place with a poodled hedge resembling float orbs, a sure sign that Sunny Hirose used a Japanese gardener. Mas had to give the man credit for that.

They stood on his porch and rang his doorbell. They already knew someone was at home, because the closed cur-tains had parted for a second as they came up the walkway.

The door opened, revealing a man about Mas's age. He was a head taller, with a huge, round face. He looked run-of-the-mill, aside from a huge abalone-shell pendant hang-ing around his neck.

"We lookin' for Sunny Hirose," Mas said.

"I'm Sunny Hirose."

"You speak Japanese?" Mas spouted out, hoping that his translator role could be dispensed with.

"No," Sunny said, a little too emphatically. "Just a few

phrases."

Yuki stepped forward. "I am Kimura. Yuki Kimura. I work with Itai-*san* back in Tokyo."

"Really? He was a lone ranger. Please, come in. Sorry for the mess. When I closed my jewelry store, I had to move everything in here."

The interior of the house was nothing like the exterior. It was stuffed with random objects that clashed and confused Mas. An iron sat on the fireplace mantel, next to a Christmas elf. Never mind that it was the middle of March. There were dusty packages of chocolate macadamia nuts on the floor, next to about five containers of automotive oil.

"Did you work with my cousin's son, too?" Sunny asked Mas, while he removed a stack of *Rafu Shimpo* newspapers from one of his chairs.

"No. I'zu Mas Arai."

"Mas. I think I've seen you before. You connected with the credit union?" Sunny went over to another chair, which was loaded up with packages of toilet paper, and attempted to clear another place to sit.

Mas shook his head.

"Bay City Gardeners' Association over on Sawtelle Boulevard?"

Yuki was obviously tiring of the twenty questions directed as Mas. "Arai-*san* is gardenah," he said, "but not here."

"Pasadena, San Gabriel," Mas finally interjected.

"Oh, out that way. That's pretty far."

"Arai-*san* is my driver. And translator."

"You drink *ocha*?" Sunny asked. "I'm an old bachelor, but I can still make a cup of green tea."

"Yes, but—" Yuki started to say, but before he could finish his sentence, the old man disappeared through his stacks of boxes.

Mas was not the king of housekeeping himself, but with three additional people in his home, he had become more particular. Sometimes one unwashed spoon or plate in the sink could set him off. In the past, it was fine because it was his own mess, but now he often found someone else's mess to be completely intolerable.

This mess of a house was Sunny Hirose's. It had nothing to do with Mas, so he tried to keep it that way in his head. Still, he refused to take a seat, afraid that a pile of magazines would fall on his head.

Yuki used Sunny's absence to snoop around. He studied a trophy on top of the mantel next to the Christmas elf and some crooked framed photos on the wall behind boxes of soy sauce. Over in the corner was a large piece of equipment, a tabletop with a metal sander attached to it. Mas, who'd done his share of woodworking, had seen something like that before but couldn't remember where.

Sunny finally returned with two steaming mugs, a tea-bag string hanging from each one. He wore thick gold rings—Mas could make out the words, "Korea" and "Army" on a couple of them.

"You play *beisuboru*," Yuki said after accepting one of the mugs.

"What?"

"Baseball," Mas interpreted.

"You have photos." Yuki pointed to the framed photos.

"Oh, yeah. Me and my older brother. A lifetime ago. When we were in camp. Does he know what that is?"

Mas turned to Yuki and asked whether he was aware of the camps that imprisoned Japanese Americans during World War II.

Yuki nodded, but Mas had his doubts about whether the Hiroshima-born man really understood.

"I was in Gila River. Had a pretty good team there." Sunny turned his attention back to Mas. "What camp were you in?"

"I'zu not in camp. In Japan."

"Oh," Sunny said. Now that Mas had said Japan, Sunny seemed totally disinterested. Some Nisei had no idea what it was like overseas during World War II: the firebombings over Tokyo, the hunger in their bellies that could barely be sated by sweet potatoes, the black rain over a decimated city. There was no sense in mentioning Hiroshima, because that's not why they were there in Sawtelle.

"Anyway, what can I help you with?"

"Itai-*san*," Yuki said, "did he seem bothered by anything while he was here?"

Mas attempted to translate the best he could.

"Well, you worked with him. You know what he was like. Never slept. Always on his phone or on the computer. It was no wonder that he dropped dead like that. He was married to his work. I told him it would be better if he settled down, got married. Don't be like me. But he told me that no woman would be able to stand him. I guess he was right."

Yuki's back straightened when Sunny spoke of Itai's phone and computer. Mas could guess what Yuki's next question would be. Sure enough, he asked, "Are the computer and phone still here?"

"The phone, I don't know, but the police took away his computer yesterday. You can go into the room he was using and see what's left."

This room was as bare as a prison cell compared to the living room: just a small twin mattress topped with a nylon sleeping bag, and a television tray that probably served as a makeshift desk.

Yuki leafed through the papers on the TV tray. They were all computer printouts in Japanese. "This is a list of the players on the Japan team."

Not surprising, Mas thought. *Wasn't that what the reporter was here for?*

"Can you ask whether he has a computer printer? Did Itai-*san* use it?"

Mas interpreted and Sunny responded, "Yes, in fact, he did. He gave me a file on those what-you-call-it…thumb drives. I think I may still have it." When he went to retrieve it, Mas wandered into the attached bathroom. It replicated the living room's discordant look. A shelf that was probably designed for toiletries held about ten boxes of baseball bobble-head dolls. An open hamper revealed not dirty clothes but shoe boxes.

On the tile counter Mas saw shaving cream, a used disposable razor, a toothbrush, and Japanese toothpaste, squeezed from the middle. He didn't see any prescription medicine, although based on the rings in the medicine chest, there once were some.

Sunny appeared in the bathroom's doorway and handed over the thumb drive, a simple gray rectangle.

"Itai-*san* take medicine, *desho*?" Yuki asked directly.

"High blood pressure. Runs in the Itai family. I have it, too."

"Youzu see him take it?"

"If you mean his pills, yes. He usually carried them with him, though. Why?"

Yuki nudged Mas. "Ask him if someone has access to his house. Or if anyone has come over."

Mas frowned. "Like who, a housekeeper?"

"Just ask."

Mas did.

"No, it's just me," Sunny responded. "I mean, I have a poker game here every Friday night with my old buddies from the Korean War. But that's about it."

After a few more circles of Itai's space, Yuki nodded that he was ready to go.

"Sah, thank you, *ne*." Mas was genuinely appreciative. Not many men his age would be this accommodating.

"You guys take it easy," Sunny said, taking hold of the half-empty mugs.

"Again, very sorry about Itai-*san*." Yuki bowed before he left. As they made their way back to the Impala, he hissed in Mas's ear: "I think he knew more Japanese than he let on."

"Could be," Mas replied. It was hard to figure out

the Nisei and their attitudes about speaking their parents'
language.

Back in the passenger seat, Yuki pulled out a digital tablet from his computer bag. Slipping the thumb drive into
one of its ports, he tapped the screen here and there. Mas
watched as Japanese text appeared on the screen.

"Itai-*san* was collecting dirt on practically every player
on the team."

"You don't seem too bothered that this Itai's dead," Mas
said to his passenger in Japanese.

"Of course, I'm upset. He was my *senpai*. Practically my
mentor. Taught me everything about research, writing good
stories. That's why I'm here."

Still, Mas thought Yuki's emotional responses this
whole time seemed muted. It was all about the story. As he
started the Impala, he glanced back at the neat ranch-style
house, its exterior masking the chaos within.

★ ★ ★

While Mas was driving east on the 10, the cell phone in his
pocket went off.

"What's that? You mean you have a cell phone, *Ojisan*?"

Mas didn't bother to reply. Once he braked to a stop for
traffic, Mas pulled it out to see who had called.

"Ge—neh—see." Yuki looked over Mas's shoulder.
"What kind of name is that?"

Mas returned the phone to his pocket. The last thing he
wanted to talk about with the boy was Genessee.

"I'm hungry," Yuki said when they were passing downtown L.A.'s skyscrapers.

So was Mas.

"Anywhere to eat near Dodger Stadium?"

There was nothing directly around Chavez Ravine. But on the edge of Chinatown was Philippe's, a Dodger Blue haunt. It was the historic home of the French dip sandwich: slices of beef, pork, lamb, or turkey soaked in meat *jus* and stuffed in a long bun that had been dipped into the savory jus. Add just a dab of custom-made hot mustard, and you were set.

Yuki brought his tablet into the restaurant—which was smart, since you never knew when robbers would do a smash-and-dash in the parking lot. After they ordered their sandwiches at the counter from a waitress wearing a little blue cap on her head, they carried their trays past long tables of uniformed cops, office workers wearing laminated badges, and men in baseball caps. The heels of their shoes crunching on the sawdust on the floor, they finally found an empty wooden booth in the corner.

Mas chowed down on his lamb dip, but Yuki was more interested in his tablet screen. "*Souuuuu*," he finally said. He leaned back in the booth and took his first bite of his sandwich. "The date on this computer file. It's from three days ago. Right when he arrived."

What of it? Mas thought.

"There's dirt on here, but it's all things we already suspected."

"Maybe more on his laptop?" Mas asked.

"Probably." Yuki then cursed. "I hoped this thumb drive would hold all the answers."

They finished off their lunch with gulps of Coke and left. Only twenty minutes until the press conference—Mas sped up the hilly streets to the stadium. A press representative was waiting for them at the top of the stadium's stairs and directed them to the elevator. They joined another journalist in the elevator down to the Tommy Lasorda room.

Mas stood in the back of the room, while Yuki sat at the end of the second row. Mas saw the same cast of press characters: the sleepy-looking cameramen, the Japanese reporters in suits, and the Latino photographer who had helped Itai.

"You're back. Mas Arai, right?" said a familiar gravelly voice next to him.

Mas grunted. It was one of the detectives who had questioned him a couple of days earlier.

"Back to the scene of the crime."

Just what was this *aho* saying to him?

"Or, I guess, the scene of what we think was a crime. The coroner is still working on the toxicology report. These things take time, I guess."

In fact, the *hakujin* man up front was saying the same thing. "We're waiting for the results from the coroner's office. As soon as we hear from them, we'll hold another press conference for the Japanese media. So please refrain from contacting us in the meantime." He then stopped talking and let an interpreter translate his message.

Based on his scowl, Yuki was not impressed. He was furiously tapping his pen on his notebook, as if he could barely stay seated.

"Why is the head person not here to speak to us? A member of our press corps was killed in this stadium, and we need to hear directly from him," he practically shouted in Japanese. "I'm Kimura Yuki with *Nippon Series,* and it was my colleague who met his sad demise here."

While the baseball executive listened to the English translation from the interpreter at his side, Yuki turned to his colleagues. "I'm shocked by your response. Or lack of response. Itai-*san*'s killer is at large. Any of you could be the next victim. Maybe the killer is in this room."

The reporters let out audible sighs; it was obvious that no one took Yuki seriously. Mas sincerely felt badly for him, but having an outburst like this seemed less than professional.

"Again, we are sorry for your colleague's passing, and we are certainly working with the authorities to get answers. We'll inform all of you as soon as we hear anything definitive."

The reporters got up, making sure not to make eye contact with Yuki. Only the young blonde, April Sue, approached Yuki, taking down his contact information and giving him her business card. Smitty Takaya wasn't there; this probably had nothing to do with his area of responsibility, but Mas missed that shock of white hair and his easygoing demeanor. The female broadcast reporter, Amika, was also absent. She probably knew that the press conference would be a waste of time.

Mas left the press conference first, figuring that Yuki

had enough interpreters, professional ones, to come to his aid. Also, he wanted to stay clear of that detective. What was he doing here, anyway? Was it like Yuki has said—maybe the killer was someone in the press corps?

Because the follow-up game was tomorrow, some Japanese players were out in the wide hallway. A couple were cleaning their teeth with toothpicks; they'd probably just finished their afternoon meal down the hall. Yuki finally emerged, and when he saw Neko Kawasaki walking toward him, his face visibly softened.

"Hello," he said.

"Hello."

"It's been a while."

"Only six months."

"You've been pitching well."

"So you've been following?"

"Watching on the internet when I can."

"I need to go back to Hawaii soon."

"I'm in Sho Tokyo. At the Miyako."

"Oh, I'm at the Bonaventure downtown."

"Bonaventure—oh, that's famous."

"It's old. I think that it was built in the 1970s."

This conversation was complete nonsense. Mas finally approached Yuki and murmured in Japanese, "Let's go."

But Yuki would not be deterred from his mission. "Dinner. Tonight."

"Not sure if that's a good idea. I don't think the team manager wants us to socialize with reporters. Especially someone from *Nippon Series*."

"I won't ask you anything about Itai."

Neko rolled her eyes.

"Well, you don't have to answer them then."

"If it only would be that easy."

"You have your same cell phone number, right? I'll call you later."

"You can try. I can't stop you from trying." Neko walked away, bobbing her head toward Mas before disappearing into the women's restroom.

Mas shook his head, not believing what he'd just witnessed.

"What? What?"

"Embarrassing," Mas said in Japanese.

"What do you mean?"

"Sheezu not interested," he stated plainly in English.

"How do you know?"

Mas heard the tapping of high heels against concrete, and then a swirl of yellow appeared in front of them. "So I see the *Nippon Series* has sent another one of its loser dogs to America. I guess they're more desperate than I thought." It was Amika, wearing a dress the color of the center of a daisy.

Yuki cringed. Mas knew that Yuki had a sharp tongue, and so she was surprised that he didn't use it against the broadcast reporter. "I'm just here to cover a story. Just like you."

"No, what we do is report. Not spread unsubstantiated gossip." She turned and clicked away.

"She just can't let it go," Yuki murmured.

"What?" Mas asked, but the boy pretended not to hear him. Their drive back to the Little Tokyo hotel was quiet, which suited Mas just fine. He was beginning to realize that this so-called journalist's trip to Los Angeles may be about more than just his dead colleague. Perhaps a female knuckle-ball pitcher.

After Mas dropped Yuki off, he got on his cell phone. Genessee deserved more than he had offered last night.

When she opened her front door, she looked fresh and bright-eyed. And yes, maybe beautiful. Mas felt a tingle in his limbs.

"How was your day?" she asked, offering him a glass of red wine.

"Orai if we don't talk about it?"

Genessee smiled, revealing the tiny gap in her teeth. "Of course."

Chapter Five

The next morning, Mas checked his cell phone as best he could. As far as he could tell, only one message. From Mari.

Walking out of Genessee's bedroom through the sliding glass doors and into her backyard, he carefully pressed the button to call back.

"Hallo."

"Dad, where are you?"

"Genessee's house."

"Oh. You haven't been staying over there lately, so we didn't know where you were."

It wasn't what Mari thought. Genessee had filled Mas up with lasagna and garlic bread after he'd stopped by last night. It was the wine that had done it. The last thing he remembered was sitting back on her couch while something was on the television. How he'd ended up in Genessee's bed, he didn't know. He was stripped down to his T-shirt but was still wearing his jeans.

Mas didn't say a word. How many times was Mari

missing from her room during her summers in between college semesters? By that time, Chizuko was gone; communication had all but broken down between father and daughter.

"You have to call, Dad. Just check in so we know that you're safe."

"Yah, yah." He knew she was right, but again, it hadn't been his intention to stay the night on the westside. It was already nine in the morning. And no call from Yuki yet. "Anybody callsu me?"

"No. Who were you expecting? That Yuki dude?" She pronounced his name like "yucky"—on purpose, Mas figured.

"I'zu be home tonight. No *shinpai*."

"I'm making dinner. You can invite Yuki, if you want."

Mas grimaced. His little girl wasn't much of a cook. But he knew she was being gracious, so he accepted the invitation as best he could.

After he got off of the phone, he walked toward Genessee's rock garden. The one he'd created for her about five years ago. He'd picked up the larger rocks from the Imperial Valley. One was shaped like the giant head of an eagle. All in all, the garden was holding up well, even though the occasional bird chose to splatter its white gifts onto the rocks.

It needed to be raked periodically, and Mas had purchased a special metal one for this purpose. He knew that the *hakujin* pictured a Zen priest in a robe doing such raking in a meditative state—not a white-T-shirted old man with morning breath. And while a priest might think of the fragility of life while he raked, Mas was pondering murder.

Who hated Itai? The first person that came to his mind was the TV reporter, Amika Hadashi. She definitely seemed to have a bone to pick with Itai. He wasn't sure what had happened between them, but it seemed very personal. But would she attempt to kill him right in front of the entire Japanese media corps? It seemed unwise, and she struck Mas as being very clever. The catcher, Sawada, wasn't a fan of Itai's, either.

Other than those two, Mas couldn't think of any others. But Itai had said he'd be making an announcement that would rock the baseball world. What in the world could command such interest?

★ ★ ★

Mas tried Yuki's cell phone a couple of times, but no dice. He even called the Miyako Hotel, but after a few rings he was sent to the guest voicemail service. Until now, Yuki had been so eager and on the ball to get moving. Perhaps Amika Hadashi's biting words had dampened his enthusiasm.

Genessee appeared, a mug of steaming coffee in each hand. She knew the right way to start the day. Mas could imagine that this would be something he could easily get used to. He literally shook his head to erase such thinking before accepting the cup.

After coffee with Genessee, Mas was on the move. He parked the car in the Miyako's three-story structure and walked into the lobby. There was no sense in calling Yuki again, so he took the elevator to the third floor.

"Yuki," he called out, knocking his knuckle against the door. "Yuki, youzu in there? Mas here."

He heard the pitter-patter of feet and then somebody knocking into furniture.

Whatthehell was going on?

He stayed quiet for a few seconds and then tried the door. It swung open and Amika Hadashi stood on the other side. Instead of being flawlessly coiffed, her hair was mussed up, frizzy all over. Wearing the same yellow dress—only it seemed to have wilted a bit—she held a pair of high-heeled shoes.

"Ah, *ohayo*," she mouthed her good morning and then ran down the hall in her bare feet.

For a moment, Mas didn't know what to do. He, of all people, should not judge, but he did. What had the boy gotten himself into?

Yuki appeared, an unlit cigarette hanging from his lips. He wore no shirt, revealing a carriage that was muscular, despite his thin frame. On his arm was the tattoo Mas had forgotten about—a wart hog, because he'd been born in the year of the *Inoshishi*. "Come in, *Ojisan*."

Mas did.

"You have a light?" Mas shook his head.

"I quit," Mas admitted. It was after Takeo had been born.

"Too bad," Yuki said. "I think I liked you better when you smoked."

Mas let that one pass, because it was obvious that Yuki

was recovering from a hangover. His room was a complete mess. The ice tub was on the floor next to an empty bottle of whiskey and, of course, two glasses. One of them was marked by red lipstick.

Yuki pulled the crumpled sheets off the bed, revealing a shiny metal lighter. "Got it," he said, finally smiling before lighting his cigarette.

Mas was pretty sure that the hotel didn't allow smoking. But what did he care? Yuki's name was on the registry, not his. He did, however, notice the smoke alarm on the wall and pointed to it for Yuki's edification. The boy bent down to retrieve one of his shoes and aimed it toward the disk. Bam! Got it on the first try. Maybe Yuki had a future as a baseball pitcher.

Mas sat on the padded chair on wheels by the desk. Yuki, meanwhile, reclined on his unmade bed, the cigarette ash falling onto the pristine white sheets.

"*Sou*," Yuki said.

"So," Mas replied.

"Looks like Japan may be facing Korea again on Sunday."

As interesting as that statement was, Mas wasn't waiting to hear that. He wanted to know why a half-dressed Amika Hadashi had come out of Yuki's hotel room.

"Ah, shit," Yuki said. "I know you probably think I'm lying, but I really didn't expect that to happen. I actually went to the Bonaventure. To talk to Neko. I didn't have her room number, and the employees wouldn't give it to me. I called her room, and she said she couldn't talk. That she had an appointment." He tossed the cigarette stub into a glass with a line of brown liquid. "She wouldn't tell me with who. I just waited there by the elevators. Waiting for her to appear so I could just talk to her."

The boy was obviously lovesick, so sick that he looked like a pitiful fool.

"I must have fallen asleep, because suddenly she was there, shaking my shoulder. I thought I saw an angel. I really did. But the angel was with someone. Was with that Korean pitcher, Jin-Won Kim."

"Both knuckleball pitcha. Maybe talkin' about dat."

"No, this wasn't anything about knuckleballs, I'll tell you that much."

"Youzu don't know."

"No, *Ojisan*, I know. I could tell how he held her elbow. And how she leaned into him. And he's married. A kid, just a baby."

"Whatchu do?"

"I went back to Little Tokyo, to the bar across from the hotel. And then she shows up. Amika. She sits right next to me. I tried to ignore her, but how could I? The bar is filled with mostly Americans. College students. Strangers. I have no one to talk to, so I talk to her."

Mas knew what was going to happen next.

"We came back to my room."

"It looks like it," Mas said in Japanese.

"Don't judge me, okay? You're old, so you don't know how it is. She's the one who brought the whiskey."

This Amika was something else, Mas thought. For a woman to be carrying around a bottle of whiskey like that?

"She's seeing someone, you know. The catcher, Sawada."

Mas lifted his eyebrows in surprise.

"They have an open relationship," said Yuki.

"What dat mean?"

"That he gets to sleep around."

"And she?"

"Not so much," said Yuki. "He adores her. I don't know why. She's awful."

Mas frowned, confused.

"I was drunk, okay? I actually don't remember much of anything. But obviously something happened here."

Naturally.

"I don't like Amika. Not one bit." Yuki's glasses were back on his face. "She was engaged to a sumo wrestler before, you know. It was supposed to be true love. Once his star began to fall, she dropped him. Just like that."

The thin reporter with a beefy giant? Unfathomable.

"She's too old for me, anyway. And she's always digging around for stories. She's working on a big one on Neko, actually. Not sure when it's going to air, but she even interviewed Neko's parents back in Yokohama. It didn't go well; at least that's what Neko said. Her father won't even talk about it."

"So Neko-*san* your girlfriendo or sumptin?"

"Well, we did spend some time together. *Nippon Series* sent me to Hawaii to cover her a few months ago. I thought maybe, well, that we could continue where we left off. But it certainly seems like she's moved on with Jin-Won."

Yuki sat up, the ash falling onto his T-shirt. "She needs

to be careful," he said, talking to himself more than to Mas. "There's a lot of Korean media here, too. It would be terrible if they cast her as Jin-Won's mistress. It could even have international repercussions."

Mas's interest was peaked. Isn't that what Itai said? That he knew of something that would have a global impact?

Yuki stepped over his mess to make his way to the bathroom. Meanwhile, Mas rolled open the curtains to take a look down at First Street. A van was parked at the curb, and Mas recognized some of the photographers he'd seen at the first game between Japan and Korea.

The toilet flushed, and Yuki joined Mas by the window. Peering down on the street, he said, "Something is going on. Let's get down there." He rummaged for his pants and then a shirt. He couldn't seem to find anything that wasn't wrinkled into a ball. "*Ojisan*, let me wear your *Nippon Series* polo shirt? You're wearing a T-shirt underneath that, right?"

I thought I didn't look professional, Mas thought, but he took off the shirt anyway and handed it over. Looking at himself in the full-length mirror, Mas scowled. *Now I look a gardener*-san *more than ever.* He put on his jacket so he'd at least have a more professional appearance.

The two of them rushed downstairs. As they headed out through the hotel's glass door, they saw that the van was still in front. The driver was programming his GPS, while another Asian man rushed into the open vehicle, shouting instructions in a foreign language, most likely Korean.

In the jumble of foreign words, Mas and Yuki were both able to make out the destination. The Bonaventure Hotel.

Yuki pulled out his cell phone. "I need to warn her," he said, pressing down on the screen.

The lovesick boy was again overreacting. Who knew why they were headed to the Bonaventure?

"Neko-*san*. It's me. Yuki. Call me as soon as you get this," he said, his words rapid-fire. Then to Mas: "Get the car."

"Where weezu goin'?"

"Bonaventure."

"Who knowsu why they goin' ova there."

"We do this all the time, Arai-*san*," Yuki. "If our competitors are rushing off to cover a story, we follow them."

"But no idea—"

"Yes, even if we have no clue about what's happening."

Mas grit down on his dentures. No wonder the news business was in big trouble these days.

Once they parked in the expansive lot across the street from the Bonaventure and entered the hotel, Mas and Yuki faced a maze of escalators and elevators. A collection of reflective cylinders near the 110 Freeway, the Bonaventure reminded Mas of high-tech urban silos, but instead of grain, they held human strangers to Los Angeles. The silos were old, built in the mid-seventies, but they'd aged surprisingly well. Or maybe they were like palm trees—originally from an alien place, but now solidly part of the L.A. landscape.

They found a video screen with a list of that day's hotel events: a meeting of community college administrators, a gathering of doctors, and then, yes, a press conference in a banquet room on the second floor. Some familiar-looking

Asian journalists were heading up the carpeted stairs, so Mas and Yuki followed all the way to one of the banquet rooms.

Jin-Won Kim was seated behind a covered table in front of a few rows of padded chairs. TV cameras were set up and ready to roll.

Yuki didn't seem to recognize anyone—that is, until a woman in a flowing peach blouse stepped in front of him.

"What are you doing here?" he asked Amika.

"I was going to ask you the same thing."

Yuki didn't answer and found an empty seat on the end of the front row. Mas opted to stand in the back. Amika, unfortunately, took her place right next to Mas. He chose not to acknowledge her existence.

A woman with a camera came by. While everyone else's cameras were large and had large lenses, hers was palm-size and conventional. And what was even more interesting was that she wasn't aiming her camera at Jin-Won. No, she was taking pictures of Mas and Amika. Mas recognized her—he'd seen her on the field at Dodger Stadium before Itai had died.

"Whozu dat?" Mas grudgingly asked his neighbor against the wall.

"Sally Lee. She's not with the media. She's part of a Korean women's advocacy group."

Before Amika could elaborate, the press conference began. Sure enough, it was in Korean.

Amika seemed to understand the speaker, a middle-aged Korean man in a suit sitting next to Jin-Won.

"You knowsu Korean?" Mas asked.

"Some. I can get by."

"Whatsu goin' on?"

"Jin-Won wants to join the major leagues."

"Can he do dat?"

"He just told the Korean press that he wants to. He can be officially posted after this season. If his current team, the Unicorns, agrees."

This was certainly news to the journalists, who looked electrified. Questions shot out from various corners of the room. Yuki, who was observing carefully, nudged the man next to him, who seemed to give him an update.

During this flurry, Mas noticed two new figures standing in the doorway of the meeting room. Two women. Neko and an older woman whom Mas had seen at Dodger Stadium.

"Whozu dat ole woman?" Mas asked Amika.

"What's it to you?"

"I'zu see her before. At Dodger Stadium."

"You are very observant for a gardener."

Mas's eyes widened. Why should Amika know that he was a gardener?

"Yuki and I talked a lot last night."

That's not all you did, Mas thought.

Mas wasn't the only one to notice Neko. Yuki was out of his seat and making a beeline for her.

Not good, Mas thought. He tried unsuccessfully to divert the boy's attention.

"I didn't expect to see you here," Yuki said to Neko in Japanese.

"I'm just here to support Jin-Won."

"So is this part of your plan? He comes to America to be close to you."

Neko frowned. "I'm in Hawaii. Hawaii is closer to Korea than most of the major league teams in America. He wants competition. He wants to play in the majors."

"And I suppose his wife and baby will be back in Korea—quite convenient for the two of you."

Neko, whose pale face was as smooth as that of a white peach, scrunched it into an awful grimace, as ugly as the *oni* devil mask that once adorned the Arai hallway. She pulled one of her arms back and unleashed a slap as loud as a thunderclap across Yuki's right cheek.

"Neko!" the old woman cried out, running to the pitcher's side. She cradled Neko's hands as if they were made of fragile glass.

"No worries," the pitcher said in Japanese to the older woman. "I used my left hand."

★ ★ ★

"You gotsu to stop." Mas had pulled the boy into the hallway. He was making a complete *aho* out of himself.

"I'm in love with her," Yuki said in Japanese.

That was obvious.

"She decide to go wiz Jin-Won, datsu her decision," said Mas.

"She has a chance to become the first female major leaguer."

"Whatsu dat to you?"

"I want her to succeed. I want her to achieve her dreams."

Mas examined the boy's face. *Chikusho.* He was telling the truth. He was punch-drunk in love with that woman. "Youzu gotta get your head on straight. Find out what happen to Itai."

Yuki took a deep breath, in and out. He paced the hallways and returned to Mas. "You're right, *Ojisan.* I need you to call."

"Call who?"

"The coroner. Find out the status of the autopsy report."

"Me?" Mas said in Japanese. Was Yuki *kuru-kuru-pa*?

"You'll be better at communicating than me. You're the one who's telling me to concentrate on work."

Mas cursed. The boy was right. He couldn't get out of this one. After Yuki pressed in the number, Mas took the phone. "Hallo. I want to talk to coroner."

"What is this regarding?"

Whatthehell was Itai's first name?

"I'zu reporter. From Japan."

"You can leave a voice message with our press department."

After some clicks, Mas explained that he was leaving a message. "Dis from Yuki Kimura, *Nippon Series.* Callin' about Mista Itai. Whatsu goin' on wiz him?"

Yuki took the phone from Mas and left his cell number.

Who knew if the coroner would respond back?

Yuki agreed that it would best to leave the Bonaventure

and stay clear of both Neko and Amika. They returned to the Little Tokyo hotel, where Yuki took a proper shower and then went shopping for fresh changes of clothes. He wasn't much of a shopper, to Mas's relief, and they ended up in a tiny gift store bordering the driveway at one of Little Tokyo's Buddhist temples.

Yuki's purchases in hand, Mas gestured toward the semi-hidden temple down the skinny driveway. "They have the Hiroshima Peace Flame in there," he said in Japanese.

Yuki came to a dead stop on the sidewalk. "What do you mean, 'flame'?"

"Someone carried it from Hiroshima," Mas said, remembering an article in *The Rafu Shimpo*. "Still burning."

"Can we see it?"

Mas shrugged. He wasn't much of a Buddhist, but he knew most of the priests around town were on the mellow side. Since Buddhists were the minority in the US, their doors were always open to newcomers.

The main sanctuary was locked, so they went to a side door to find the office. The priest, wearing a white shirt and tie underneath a solid brown kimono, looked familiar to Mas. He had a long face and eyes that looked both welcoming and sad. He must have officiated at one of the many funerals that Mas seemed to attend every other weekend.

"I understand you have the Hiroshima Peace Flame here," Yuki said. "I am from Hiroshima."

"Oh, really?" the priest said, almost as if he was expecting Yuki. He led them out of the office and into the darkened sanctuary. At the side of the main altar was an ornate gold lantern shaped like a beer stein. A faint flame illuminated its center. "In the 1980s, the mayor of Los Angeles brought the flame over in ember form from the Hiroshima Peace Park," the priest said. He'd obviously told this story before.

How could he bring fire on an airplane? Mas wondered. He must have had to go through a lot of clearance for that.

Yuki put his hands together and bowed toward the light. This moment of reverence both touched and surprised Mas. The boy then stepped back and waited, as if he expected Mas to do the same. But Mas had experienced the flames of the Bomb firsthand. He felt no need to bow to it now.

As they walked back to the hotel, Mas remembered Mari's earlier offer. "Youzu can wash some of your dirty stuff at my house. My daughta invite you ova for dinner, anyways."

Yuki seemed relieved for the chance to eat a home-cooked meal. *He didn't know what he was in for,* thought Mas. Mari was still in her healthy, no-rice, no-bread mode. In other words, a big pile of various raw greens with squares of fresh tofu.

Yuki's eyes widened as he stared at the white cubes on his plate on the dining room table.

"What, is something wrong?" Mari asked as she passed around some miso dressing.

The boy was smart enough to stay silent and shake his head no. Takeo, who was raised on raw, unsalted almonds and dried cranberries, happily began to eat, and so did Lloyd.

Mas felt the last bit of fat leave his body as he bit into

the fancy organic lettuce. Just what did his daughter want—for them to be a family of skeletons?

The doorbell rang, saving him from taking another forkful of salad. "I'll get it, Dad," Mari said, pushing him back down in his seat.

Mas heard a familiar bright voice at the door and then, there she was. Genessee, with a casserole dish full of carbohydrates and cheese.

"Auntie Genessee!" Takeo called out. Even Lloyd was smiling. She was a favorite of the house, no doubt about that.

Yuki, on the other hand, looked utterly confused. He was probably taking in Genessee's Afro and dark skin. "Aunt-tee?"

"I'm Genessee Howard," she extended her hand. "*Hajimemashite*. I'm Mas's, ah—"

"That's my father's girlfriend. You know, lady friend?" Mari interjected.

Mas wished that he could sink into the floor, right then and there.

"You didn't say anything about having a girlfriend," Yuki said in Japanese to Mas. "What about my grandmother?"

"Who is his grandmother?" Mari understood at least that much Japanese.

"Akemi Kimura. We lived with Arai-*san* here."

"What's going on?" Born on a US military base in Japan, Genessee, whose mother was from Okinawa, knew enough Japanese to get by.

Just then Yuki's cell phone rang.

Good timing, Mas thought.

"Yes, waitaminute," Yuki answered, gesturing for Mas to take over.

"Hallo."

The voice on the other side was that of a man, probably a little younger than middle-aged. "This is the deputy coroner. I just want to inform Mr. Kimura about the cause of death in the case of Tomo Itai. It's definitely cyanide poisoning. Ingested a few minutes before he died." He promised to email the report to Yuki's phone.

As promised, just minutes after Mas got off the phone, the email arrived. Yuki bent over the report on his screen, mouthing out the English words. Finally, Mari couldn't stand it any longer and grabbed it away. In about thirty seconds, she'd absorbed it all. "It was cyanide, Lloyd," she told her husband. "He somehow got it into his system at the stadium."

★ ★ ★

Yuki insisted that he be driven back to the hotel immediately to continue work on his investigation into Itai's murder.

"*Hai, hai,*" Mas said, digging out his keys from his front pocket. He was really starting to regret agreeing to be the boy's driver.

Yuki was already waiting by the Impala when Genessee got in front of Mas before he was out the door.

"I don't understand, Mas. Who is that young man?"

"Heezu nobody."

"He's a journalist who is obviously investigating some kind of murder. And you look like you're involved in some way."

Mas lowered his head. *Shimmata*. He'd been found out. He knew he should have been more forthcoming to Genessee, but that would have required energy. Energy that he couldn't muster. It was easier to operate in his usual mode. Avoiding the truth.

"I'zu his driver." Mas didn't bother to add "translator," because that would have made it all the more ridiculous.

"Did you have a relationship with that woman?" she asked.

"Huh?"

"I know you can hear me perfectly well. That woman. His grandmother. Akemi Kimura."

"Same class as her brotha. Datsu all."

"Why do I think that's not all?"

Embarrassed, Mas swung his gaze back to the living room to check if any of his family members were in earshot. They must have sensed that something was amiss, because the room was empty, yet all the dirty plates remained on the table.

"Mas, what are we doing? We aren't kids. I don't need a ring around my finger, but I do need something. Honesty, for one. Do you get what I'm saying?"

Mas looked away. He felt Chizuko's spirit pressing into his chest. Out in the backyard, wilting cymbidiums were collected in the corner. If he opened his heart to Genessee, really opened it, wouldn't his decades of life with Chizuko fall and blow away like dead leaves?

"I- I- I-…" he stammered. Full words could not be formed.

"I get it, Mas," Genessee said, her chin jutting out. "I hear you loud and clear."

"*Ojisan*," Yuki called out, tapping on his watch.

"I gotsu go. Talk later?"

"Don't bother," said Genessee. "Obviously talking to me hasn't been a priority. So why change now?"

Chapter Six

"You have some secrets, too," Yuki said as Mas drove through the curves of the Pasadena Freeway. The freeway, the nation's oldest operating one, had sharp whips of turns. During the day, you could see brown hills balancing tiny homes and a collection of historic Victorians painted in ridiculous colors of the rainbow. At night, however, darkness reigned. Lights were few and far between, and Mas's headlights revealed the metal divider, scraped and dented from accidents of the past.

Mas wasn't in the mood to do true confessions in the Impala. Yuki had no right to his personal stories. They were Mas's to hold close and protect. Once they were released in the form of words, they could be mangled and distorted. And Yuki, being a journalist, was a practitioner of the black arts.

★　★　★

The next morning, thankfully, was dedicated to work.

Not Yuki's work. Real work. Gardening work for Mas's one customer, a professor at UCLA. He lived in the Hollywood Hills, at the end of a windy one-lane road with no sidewalks and hardly any guardrails. Drive off the road and you'd be flying down a dusty bluff with only an occasional yucca plant to witness your fall. During the winter the fog often fell on the Hollywood Hills like a white blanket, and if Mas left his customers' houses too late he'd have to literally inch his vehicle—before, his Ford truck and now, his Impala sedan—down the hillside, taking him a full hour to reach the populated lowlands.

Mas had found this customer, McAdams, through another professor, Koichi Kawana, who taught landscaping classes through UCLA Extension. Kawana was famous throughout not only the Southland but even the nation. He designed the largest Japanese garden in the US, the one in Missouri. He'd worked on countless gardens in Southern California, where he lived. So when he began offering classes in Westwood, Mas, surprising Chizuko and most of all himself, signed up to go.

The class was half *Nihonjin* gardeners, Japanese Americans like himself. But the other half were a mixed bag: a handful of *hakujin* retirees and more women than he had imagined. He always sat in the back and spoke to no one, except occasionally a couple of fellow gardeners with whom he was familiar. Homework was limited, but they had to submit a final project—a Japanese-style garden using the principles Kawana taught. Mas made a few false starts but finally came up with something. He began with the kidney-shape koi pond that had been at his home in Hiro-shima and added flourishes from his years in California. A sago palm. Rocks from the San Gabriel Mountains. Birds of paradise, a tropical plant that had been officially adopted by the city of Los Angeles.

Right about that time Chizuko was diagnosed with cancer, so Mas never found out how he did in the class. But then, out of the blue, years after Chizuko had passed away, he received a phone call. It was Kawana-*sensei*. Would Mas be open to working on an estate in the Hollywood Hills?

The biggest challenge with this garden was that the foundation wasn't flat. Most Japanese-style gardens were asymmetrical anyway, but to start off that way made it more difficult to move in rocks and containers of plants. There was already a bamboo thicket in the back, one that constantly multiplied. Mas always felt like he was in the jungle as he hacked back the poles.

The McAdams family didn't want to deal with a pond and fish, which would most likely attract the wild animals from the hills anyway. Mountain lions were sometimes spotted in the area, and raccoons, with their sharp, knife-like claws, were prevalent. So Mas decided to not fight the yard's slopes but instead embrace them with the addition of rocks and a special kind of moss that grew in their crevices.

His own daughter had never even seen the garden he created, and neither had his son-in-law. They were too busy with their family and daily lives, and Mas never thought of bragging about it. He usually went to do the maintenance of it solo, but today he picked up a helper, Eduardo Fuentes.

Eduardo also worked part-time for his nephew, Raul, whom Mas had once cast as a villain. Raul had taken—well, maybe even stolen—some of Mas's customers, but he'd finally realized that they were nickel-and-dime households anyway. Mas had started his career with these tiny homes, and now it was time for someone younger to take over. At almost eighty years old, Mas was finally ready to pass the baton.

Eduardo spent most of his time chopping at the wayward bamboo with his own machete while Mas raked away the twigs and fallen leaves. He'd built a wooden bridge to link the east and west sides of the garden, and he noticed that a few boards had warped, revealing rusty nails. He removed them with the claw on the back of his hammer and pounded in new replacements.

They took a break about noon, and Eduardo kindly shared half of his torta with Mas. Mas could offer only a can of Coke in return. At least it was still cold in his plastic cooler.

Eduardo knew about Lloyd's job at Dodger Stadium and was eager to hear about their fertilizing procedures and how often they watered the grass. Talk that only another gardener would appreciate. "There'su a Japanese garden ova there," Mas said abruptly.

"At Dodger Stadium?" Frown lines marked Eduardo's forehead. He chewed slowly, as if it would make his half sandwich last longer.

"Past parking lot."

"Never knew that," Eduardo said, swallowing. "Remember Fernando?"

Mochiron, Mas thought. Of course. That pudgy pitcher from Mexico—nobody thought much of him, and then he came in for another pitcher who got hurt. Pitched a shutout. And then another win and another win and another. Until he had eight straight wins and five shutouts. Los Angeles went *kuru-kuru-pa,* and Mas had to admit that he went a little crazy, too.

"Heezu good."

"Yah, he sure was."

They kept chewing their tortas there on the repaired bridge. Eduardo took a good look around. "Lookin' good, Mister Arai. Lookin' good."

★ ★ ★

After dropping Eduardo back at his house, Mas was unfortunately alone with his thoughts. He wasn't one for music, but he flipped on the radio, hoping for news of a political scandal, or an athlete breaking a record, or anything to take his mind off his personal life. FM stations didn't come in right; the Impala, like his ex-truck, the Ford, was old and had only the basics. He didn't bother to get a proper replacement for the truck. Besides, most of his gardening equipment was stored at the McAdams's house, since they were his only customer.

He hadn't slept well the night before, and the Impala wove over the lines on the Hollywood Freeway. He tried to think about Itai and who may have killed him. But his thoughts couldn't remain straight in his head. What did stay were Genessee's eyes. Her plaintive eyes telling him, "Mas, man up and tell me how you are really feeling!"

Mas guided the Impala off the freeway at the next exit. He hated to admit it, but he needed other people—dare he even say friends—to help him figure out his current predicament.

He found Antonio's right where it had been located for the past twenty years. Mas had become acquainted with the restaurant relatively recently, because of the owners' daughter, Juanita Gushiken. She was the steady girlfriend of Mas's only legal-eagle friend, G.I. Hasuike, who seemed to be playing restaurateur more than lawyer these days. Mas parked in the lot, which was shared by the local laundromat.

Getting ready to push open the restaurant's glass door, Mas saw a sign posted at eye level: "We thank our customers for your patronage for the past twenty years. We will be closing our doors on June 1."

He furrowed his brow and entered the almost-empty restaurant. Juanita was chatting with a couple sitting in the far booth. He spotted G.I.'s shaven head in the only other occupied booth and walked over. "You'zu closin'," he stated more than questioned.

G.I. turned his attention from his phone. "Mas, it's good to see you. We missed you at the baseball game. Juanita, look who's here."

Juanita flashed a smile. After busing some dirty dishes into the kitchen, she came out with some fresh bread and green spicy sauce, placing them on G.I.'s table.

"Sit down, please," she said to Mas. He complied.

Several years ago, he'd first sampled that green sauce and lived to regret it. Thinking it was guacamole, he slathered it over a slice of bread and nearly burned off his tongue. He knew better now and dipped a tiny corner of the bread into the chile sauce.

Juanita explained the restaurant's closure. "My parents are worn out. They want to take it easy. Travel some."

That made perfect sense to Mas, the gardener with his single customer.

"Actually, we're not giving it up," G.I. clarified.

Juanita nodded. "Mas, we're opening up a Peruvian restaurant in Tokyo."

Mas choked on his bread. Tokyo. That was Japan. "Youzu dunno nuttin' about Japan."

G.I. began laughing. "And you do? Mas, when was the last time you were in Japan? Or specifically in Tokyo?"

"Ah, well," he had to think. Truth be told, he'd never been in Tokyo in his life. Hiroshima was way south, and when he returned to California sixty-one years ago, he got on a boat in Kobe, also in southern Japan. "Itsu been a while."

"We went recently. Six months ago."

"I dunno dis."

"Well, you've been hanging out with Genessee. No time for your friends." Juanita smiled widely and then paused. "Waitaminute. Everything is cool with Genessee, right?"

Mas opened his mouth to answer, but no sound emanated.

Juanita scooted G.I. farther into the booth with her hip and sat down across from Mas. "What's going on? You can tell us."

G.I. again looked up from his phone. "Mas, woman problems? Not you."

The two of them kept poking and prodding, and finally it all came out. "I'zu not sure what happen. Yuki talkin' about Akemi, and then sheezu mad. Like quiet mad."

"Ooooo, the silent treatment. Not good." G.I. shuddered as if he were speaking from experience.

"Who's Yuki and…Akemi?" Juanita asked.

"Oh, yeah, is Yuki in town?" G.I. and Mas had actually first met over Yuki's legal troubles a decade earlier. "He's the grandson of Mas's old girlfriend. Her name is Akemi. Yuki's a reporter or something, right, in Japan?"

"Old girlfriend? No wonder Genessee's pissed off."

Genessee wasn't jealous of Akemi, Mas was sure of that. But she might be jealous of Mas's dead wife and the place she occupied in his heart.

"Why is this reporter in L.A. right now?" asked Juanita.

Mas explained how Yuki was investigating Itai's death. "Cyanide," Mas told the couple.

"Cyanide, holy crap," G.I. said. "That's pretty rare these days. Very underworld."

"Although didn't some cult in Japan try to use it to poison a bunch of people?" asked Juanita, who also worked as a private investigator. "Wait, let me look it up." She touched the screen of her phone and began searching. The whole world's encyclopedia in something that weighed less than a deck of cards. She announced her results. "It used to be you could get it in feed stores. Or to clean machinery, metal or something. But it's not readily available anymore."

G.I. was also consulting his phone. "Yup, that attempt to release cyanide gas in the Tokyo subway system happened in 1995. Maybe it's easier to get cyanide in Japan."

"Do you think someone brought it from overseas?" Juanita asked.

Mas had no idea. Certainly there were countless men and women who'd traveled from Japan and Korea. Could they have plotted to do this from another country?

Just then his phone began to ring.

"Look at you!" Juanita laughed. "You've joined the twenty-first century."

Mas removed his humble phone from his jeans pocket.

"Oh, I spoke too soon. The twentieth century."

Mas ignored her teasing and flipped his phone open. It was Yuki, telling him that Sunny had called to say that the police had dropped off Itai's computer at the Sawtelle house.

The last thing Mas wanted to do was get back in his car, drive to Little Tokyo, and then take the 10 to the 405, notoriously the worst vehicle intersection in the nation. It was Saturday, but these days traffic on the weekend could be just as bad as during weekday rush hour.

"Gardenin'. No drivin' work for me today," he told the reporter.

"I suppose I can get a taxi."

"Go on, get a taxi," Mas told him in Japanese. Didn't the Japanese newspapers have budgets for these kind of things?

"All right, I will."

Yuki sounded put out, but Mas was dead tired. *Hell,*

I'm close to eighty, he thought. *It's a wonder I can do what I'm doing.*

"Well, tomorrow is the game," Yuki said, emphasizing the need to arrive at the stadium on time. "The deciding one between Korea and Japan. This determines the championship."

After they agreed on a time to meet tomorrow, Mas closed his phone.

Juanita switched into waitress mode. "Do you want anything to eat? *Lomo saltada*? Ceviche?"

"*Pisco?*" G.I. said, grinning.

Mas shook his head and pulled himself up to his feet. No, absolutely no liquor at this time of day. "So you'zu really leavin'?" He repeated the same question he'd asked when he first arrived. This time he directed it to Juanita.

"Yep," Juanita answered. "Japan has a population problem—not enough people. They're happy to give long-term visas to those of us with Japanese blood."

"Even if we are the ugly stepchildren," G.I. added. "Hey, you should visit us sometime in Tokyo."

Juanita gave a toothy grin. "Really, Mas, really. Don't look so sad. You know nothing stays the same."

★ ★ ★

Before Mas left Antonio's, Juanita squeezed his forearm and whispered, "Call her. I'm sure if you tell her how you feel about her, she won't stay mad."

Mas sat in the Impala for a good five minutes, watching

mothers and their young children carrying baskets of clothing into the laundromat. He wasn't sure what he was going to say, but he knew he couldn't keep silent. Every day that passed without any contact with Genessee meant it would be that much harder to reopen the closed door to their relationship. He flipped open his phone and pressed Genessee's name. The phone rang and rang until her voice came on—not her live voice, but a recorded one. She spoke slowly, definitively, as if each word was essential and important. Mas couldn't leave a message. His attempt would be an embarrassment, evidence that he should be forgotten and not pursued.

Mas was hoping to avoid any discussion of his relationship with Genessee when he arrived home on McNally Street, but no such luck. Mari was waiting for him, ready to pounce. "What happened last night, anyway?" she asked as she scooped rice into a small bowl for her father. "Genessee didn't look too happy with you."

"Nuttin'."

"Dad, you know it's okay. You can get married again. Genessee is good for you."

Mas thought he'd be relieved that his daughter was giving him permission, but it actually made him feel worse. "Whyzu I get marry again? I'zu ole man."

"Haruo did it. And he seems very happy for it."

"Anyways, wiz you all in my house, no room for nuttin' else," Mas declared, causing Mari's mouth to drop open. He was sure she'd have something to say to that, but rice or no rice, he wasn't going to stick around the kitchen to find out.

Chapter Seven

The next day, Mas was ready. He didn't have the same *Nippon Series* polo shirt, but he had a similar type that he'd gotten free at a pesticide workshop. He figured that Yuki wouldn't notice the dead-garden-snail insignia, especially as it was covered by his jacket, and he was right.

As soon as he got in Mas's car at their rendezvous spot in Little Tokyo, the boy opened the laptop he was carrying and announced, "I know why Itai-*san* was killed."

Mas felt like a stone dropped into his gut.

"This is big, *Ojisan*, bigger even than baseball itself."

Isn't that what Itai had said? That he had information that would shake up international relations?

Mas continued driving up through Chinatown, passing a newsstand manned by an old Asian man wearing a cap.

"It's about Jin-Won. The old lady who we saw at the press conference at the Bonaventure? That's his grandmother."

Mas waited to hear more. Surely that in itself wasn't earth-shaking.

"She's reported to have been an *ianfu*."

Mas had heard or read that Japanese word, *ianfu*, maybe a few times on television from Japan. Here in America, people said "comfort women." They were women, mostly from Korea and other Asian countries, who were taken to provide sex for Japanese soldiers during World War II. Had the Korean woman who'd said "*konnichiwa*" to him in Dodger Stadium endured such an experience? She looked like an ordinary Asian grandmother. But then didn't Mas and Haruo fall in the same category? Who could have imagined that they had survived the beast of the Bomb and the black rain that followed?

Mas couldn't put words to his thoughts, but it didn't really matter. Yuki would fill up the Impala just fine with words of his own. "She hasn't gone public yet, but Itai-*san* believed that she was going to announce it here in Los Angeles."

"Don't make sense," Mas murmured. Wouldn't she do that in her home country?

"Itai-*san* wanted to be the first to break the news. There's not many of them left anymore. The *Nippon Series* is one of Japan's more liberal publications, you know. Even more liberal than the *Asahi Shimbun*."

Mas didn't know about such things. Besides the TV broadcasts, all he read was the Japanese American newspaper in Los Angeles, *The Rafu Shimpo*. Yuki went on to explain that the newspapers in Japan, along with the politicians, were in a sense at war with this issue. "Some maintain that the women went along willingly to make money. That they were prostitutes."

Mas frowned. That grandmother in the Korean jacket looked about his age. What fifteen-, sixteen-year-old would volunteer for such a miserable fate? He felt sick to his stomach.

"On Itai-*san*'s calendar on this computer, it says he was supposed to meet someone after the first Japan-Korea game. He didn't say who, but he wrote that it was related to a 'book publisher.'"

A publisher about the *ianfu*?

"This is not something to take lightly. You should see what these people write on the internet," Yuki added. "The mayor of Nagasaki was shot some years ago by a nationalistic fanatic. You never know what some of these people will do."

Mas felt shivers go down his spine.

"But he wasn't killed," the reporter clarified.

And that's supposed to make me feel better? Mas was beginning to regret agreeing to help Yuki in the first place.

"Some files in here have been erased, too," Yuki said, looking at the laptop screen. "There's an empty folder called '*Gurippu*.' I wonder what that's about."

Maybe "grip" in English?

Yuki was on the same wavelength. "Maybe Itai was looking into baseball-bat grips. I'm not sure. He was a diehard baseball fan, though. Came out for spring training to see all the Japanese players on the major league teams. Sometimes he toured the minor leagues and even the independent leagues."

"Hawaii too?"

Yuki closed Itai's laptop. "I know what you're getting at, *Ojisan*. Neko had nothing to do with Itai. Or his death."

Since they got to Dodger Stadium a few hours early, Mas had no problem getting a special press parking space. As he got out of the car, he noticed Yuki bringing Itai's laptop. "Youzu takin' dat wiz you?"

"I can't let anything happen to it."

Mas had a very bad feeling about the computer. It held secrets that even empires might kill for.

Once they were on the press-box level, Yuki said, "Go get something to eat, Arai-*san*. I'll be back soon."

In the distance, Mas saw the two detectives walking toward them, and he was only too happy to avoid another encounter with them.

Mas had actually eaten at Dave's Diner, the press-box dining room for special people, once with Lloyd and Mari. He felt funny going in there, but he had an official pass, compliments of *Nippon Series*. He just wished he wasn't wearing a polo shirt advertising a pesticide that kills snails.

Pork chops were on the menu, and Mas chose that, along with mashed potatoes and lentil soup. Having come straight from Japan, Chizuko had been a terrible cook at the beginning of their marriage, but she eventually mastered potatoes and red meat. Pork chops were her specialty. He was savoring Chef Dave's version when a thin giant sat down at his table. It was the pitcher with the strange Arabian-sounding name. Soji Zahed.

"So you're a reporter, too," Zahed said. Close up, he

looked more Japanese to Mas. It wasn't only the curve of his eyes but the shape of his mouth. And, of course, he was also speaking impeccable Japanese, much better than Mas's.

"No, I just drive," Mas said.

"Oh. But you knew Itai-*san*."

Mas shook his head.

"Your friend has Itai-*san*'s computer, I noticed. Where did he get it?"

"You familiar with Itai's computer?"

"Well, he had that funny sticker on the back of it. It had the Japanese characters '*teia*.'"

Depending on how it was written, *teia* could have different meanings. Zahed borrowed a pen and napkin from the kitchen staff and wrote it down for Mas. 帝亜

Mas studied it. *Curious.* It could mean "emperor of Asia" or something like that. He didn't notice that writing on the back of the laptop. He'd have to check.

"Police finished taking a look," Mas finally told him. "Why, you worried about it?"

"No, nothing like that. Just wondered if they know what happened to Itai-*san*. He was my friend."

Mas was astonished. How could this mixed-race teen have anything in common with a *kuso*-head like Itai?

"I went to his same high school in Kyoto. Ryukokudai Heian. It's a baseball powerhouse."

Even Mas had heard of it. His own school in Hiroshima had its own impressive baseball reputation, always performing well in Japan's World Series for high school students. But the Kyoto school, he grudgingly admitted, had an even more stellar reputation.

"He's been writing about me ever since junior high school."

Mas didn't know quite what to make of Itai. He had a terrible personality yet he was obviously a *hatarakimono*, hard worker. He had always admired anyone who put sweat into his job, no matter what it might be.

"Not everyone was supportive. You know how Japan is. Hard to be a *hafu* over there. Especially as a kid."

Mas didn't ask Zahed what his non-Japanese half was. None of his business, he figured.

But Zahed volunteered the information anyway. "My dad's Iranian. Operates a little corner store in Kyoto with my mother. Itai-*san* knew my parents. They were shocked by his death. I still can't believe it."

Mas wondered if Yuki knew of Itai's close relationship with Zahed. He hadn't mentioned it before.

Just then the Latino photographer wearing his trademark vest joined them at the table. He had a pile of lettuce on his plate, which was a surprise. Mas would have guessed that the large-framed man was a cheeseburger-type guy.

The photographer sensed what Mas was thinking. "Diabetes runs in the family," he said with a sad smile.

"Well, see you later then," Zahed said to Mas in Japanese and got up.

"Tall guy." The photographer watched Zahed leave before taking a bite of his lettuce. After a few chews and a wipe of his mouth with a napkin, he said, "It's been a wild series, hasn't it? Just spoke to the detectives. For the second time."

"Oh, yah." Mas hoped they wouldn't find him again.

"Told them the exact same thing that I told them the first time. I saw him take his pill. Right before he collapsed. Took it right out of his suit pocket."

Sunny was telling the truth then. Itai carried his pills with him.

"He told me he always takes his medicine at the same time. Seven o'clock in the morning, Tokyo time. Which makes it, what, around three here in L.A. We ate together that afternoon. In this room, in fact. Nobody seemed to want to sit with him. Not well liked by other reporters, I guess."

"Whatchu talk about?"

"Nothing much, really. Our health problems. He did ask me some questions."

Mas finished his soup but kept dipping his spoon in the empty bowl.

"About why I worked for a Japanese American newspaper. And that he was curious about the Japanese over here. The Nisei specifically. He wanted to know where their allegiances would fall. Japan or America. America, I told him."

Mas hadn't picked up a napkin, so he wiped his mouth with the side of his hand.

"Are you Nisei?" the photographer asked.

Mas nodded. "I'zu Nisei. Kibei Nisei."

"The ones who were born here and went to Japan for their education. I know about you guys."

Mas wasn't sure what he was insinuating by saying "you guys."

"So what do you think? Am I right?" Another bite of

lettuce.

Mas didn't know why people asked these kinds of questions. What did it matter whether he felt American or not? Didn't change anything. He was more interested in what happened the day that Itai died.

"So after he eat, heezu orai?"

"Well, I had to get going to check the flash on my camera. One of the baseball players actually came by to talk to him when I was leaving. He didn't seem too happy."

Mas jerked his head up. Which player?

"It was the Japanese guy with the blond dye job. What's his name? Tanji?"

★　★　★

Yuki never made it to Dave's Diner. Mas got tired of waiting; besides, he felt like he stuck out like a sore thumb. After the photographer left, there were only bigshots at the other tables. Bigshots who Mas revered. It was surreal to even be in the same room as them.

Mas stumbled out of the restaurant and almost crashed into another old man. Smitty Takaya. "Mas! Good to see you again. Looking forward to the game this afternoon?" Smitty looked exactly the same as the time Mas had met him. Dazzling white hair, perfect dentures, and an erect back. He could have been in a television commercial for hemorrhoid suppositories or retirement annuities.

"Yah," Mas lied.

"I think Japan has a good chance to sew this whole

thing up."

"Dat pitcha, Jin-Won, gonna leave Korea for the majors, huh?"

Smitty, for a moment, was tongue-tied, as if he'd underestimated Mas's inside-baseball knowledge. "Well, we'll have to see what happens. The Unicorns will have to agree to release him." For some reason, Smitty didn't seem thrilled with that possibility.

Tanji, his yellow hair hidden under his baseball cap, passed by with a couple of Asian men in suits. They were trailed by two others in street clothes.

"Tanji's entourage," Smitty commented. "They're always making special requests for the highest-quality green tea for Tanji. I even had to go to Little Tokyo myself to buy it."

Soka, Mas muttered to himself. That was a superstar *senshu*'s life. Mas had even witnessed that in some of his celebrity customers' daily activities. It wasn't coffee made in a common percolator or a can of Folgers and a Mr. Coffee machine, but fancy contraptions with freshly ground whole beans. Now even regular people like his own daughter and son-in-law had taken on these practices. A chance to feel like a rich bigshot, at least for the time it took to drink a cappuccino.

"Youzu see Lloyd?" Now that Yuki was busy with whatever, Mas thought he might as well check up on the boy.

Smitty informed him that he was out on the field, and after Mas grunted his goodbye and walked away, he heard another voice behind him: "Mr. Arai."

Mas turned. Ah, *tsukammata!* He was caught by those

detectives again.

"We were just talking to your associate, Yuki Kimura," said Cortez Williams, this time wearing a bright orange tie. His partner, Garibay, the older detective with the unruly hair, looked like he was in the same clothes that he wore earlier in the week.

Associate? Mas cursed. *When does being a driver make me an associate?*

"He claims that he arrived at your house on Wednesday evening, the day after Mr. Itai died. Can you confirm that?"

Mas nodded his head. "Yah, he come." *Sonofagun. Is Yukikazu a suspect?*

"And how exactly do you know Mr. Kimura?" Williams continued.

"My friendsu grandson."

"And he happens to be a reporter with the same publication as Mr. Itai?"

Mas nodded again.

"Hell of a coincidence," Detective Garibay finally chimed in.

Mas left out the part that Yuki actually sought him out because of his and Lloyd's connection to Dodger Stadium. He shrugged his shoulders. What did the *hakujin* say? "Small world"?

"I gotsu go help with field," Mas lied.

"Well, don't let us stop you," Detective Garibay said. Mas felt the sarcasm ring in his ears.

He escaped into the elevator and went downstairs. All those knuckleheads—the police detectives, baseball players, groupies and all—were beginning to suffocate him. As the elevator doors opened and he stepped out onto the field, Mas was able to regain his equilibrium.

The turf at Dodger Stadium was a beautiful thing. The grass was living and breathing, roots stretching down into the ground where Jews were once buried in the 1800s. Mas learned from Lloyd that the sod was actually raised in Palm Desert, a Bermuda grass overseeded with rye grass to get that perennial green sheen. But it wasn't like the dye some flower growers used in standing water to get their carnations to be green for St. Patrick's Day. This concoction was natural hocus-pocus, not fake.

Lloyd's crew was connecting their long, heavy-duty hoses to the water supply to make sure the field had enough moisture. Lloyd himself was checking a spot out in left field. Mas knew enough about baseball and gardening that you had to make sure the turf was uniform. One dry spot and the ball could bounce in a different direction, perhaps even determining a win or a loss.

Mas walked along the dirt sideline. During the World Baseball Classic games, security was more relaxed than at regular Dodger games. His special ID was around his neck, but no one gave him a second look. He was just an old Japanese man to them. Utterly toothless. And if they thought that, they would be most certainly correct.

He raised his hand in acknowledgment to Lloyd, and Lloyd tipped his cap back. As Mas approached the storage area for the greenskeeping equipment, he noticed something white stuck underneath the bullpen gate. He bent down to pull it out. A baseball, but not a regular major league one. This one had some Japanese writing on it—actually, upon closer inspection, it had an imprint of a signature, but not of a baseball *senshu*. No, this one was the commissioner of the Japanese professional baseball league. *Funny that such a ball would be brought over here*, Mas thought. For these international competitions, especially with Japan versus Korea, a ball from Japan would never be allowed. He didn't know what to do with the ball. Give it to the Japanese manager or one of the coaches? Mas wasn't on that high level to have that kind of interaction. He'd just give it to Lloyd. Maybe Takeo would end up being the recipient of the wayward ball from Japan.

Stuffing the ball in his jacket pocket, Mas continued to watch the greenskeeping crew work. All of them were young and *genki*, with knees that worked and shiny eyes and hair. They had their whole lives ahead of them.

Lloyd, sweat running down the sides of his face, finally made his way to Mas. "If you want to be with your reporter friend, you better go now to the press box. The game will be starting."

"Nah, I stay wiz you guysu." The greenskeeping crew was the closest thing to his people in this place.

They sat amid lawnmowers and fertilizer carts in the storage area, the familiar scent of chemicals and dung permeating the space. A large-screen TV broadcast images of the Korean players taking the field, but the audio was turned off. Instead, an old-fashioned boom box provided the audio—the legendary Vin Scully. Scully's voice immediately soothed Mas, a familiar balm that eased the discomforts of the past few days.

Both Mas and Chizuko had been fans of John Wooden, the legendary UCLA basketball coach. Vin Scully was in the same class. The highest class, as far as Mas—and L.A. sports fans—were concerned. The longtime Lakers basketball announcer, the late Chick Hearn, was more colorful, full of sayings that made Chizuko, an immigrant, scratch her head. Hearn, who'd also hosted a bowling competition show on a local TV channel, was like a trumpet squawking in a jazz improvisation, while Vin Scully was more melodious, a wind instrument made from aged oak.

Korea started strong. They got a run across in the first inning. By the seventh-inning stretch, Korea had tacked on two additional runs, taking a 3-0 lead. But in the eighth, Uno-*san* sent two men home with a triple down the line. The score was 3-2, with Korea still on top.

It was the bottom of the ninth, and if Korea kept Japan from scoring, they'd have the win. The knuckleball pitcher and closer, Jin-Won, was in the bullpen, warming up his arm. But he never appeared. Instead, Mas saw a short, stocky pitcher running to the mound.

Vin Scully handled the switch with aplomb, introducing the player who was taking Jin-Won's place. While the spectators didn't seem to catch on, Mas knew immediately that something was seriously wrong.

Chapter Eight

Unfortunately for Korea, Jin-Won's replacement was a straight-ahead fastball pitcher, and both Tanji and Uno easily got on base for Japan. Sawada, the catcher and also Amika's boyfriend, was swinging now. Mas expected Sawada to go for a big hit, but he wisely hit a sacrifice bunt. He was out on first, but only after Tanji and Uno advanced to second and third. Next at bat was the tall *hapa* pitcher, Soji Zahed. On the television screen, he looked nervous. Vin Scully even mentioned Zahed's pitching woes on his minor league team. "Back in Japan, he was a Nippon-Ham Fighter who had an extraordinary rookie year, with eight wins and only two losses," Scully said. "He did well today. If he could only take some of that magic back to his team in Rancho Cucamonga."

Zahed swung at a ball, missing completely. Even Mas could see that his timing was off. Pretty soon it was a full count. The Korean cowbells were ringing throughout the stadium, while the Japanese fans were cheering in unison. Sitting there practically underground, Mas felt the walls shake. If Zahed got a hit and Tanji made it to home plate, Japan would at least tie. If he got at least a double, Uno would score and Zahed would win the game for Japan. Mas felt bad for the boy; he probably wasn't even twenty years old. Quite a lot of stress to place on the shoulders of a teen.

Zahed licked his lips, stuck out his *oshiri,* and held up his bat. The pitcher contorted on the mound and released the ball. Zahed swung and made contact. The ball rolled down into an empty place on left field. Tanji made a run for home from third base, with Uno right behind him. Japan had won.

"*Yatta!*" Mas was on his feet, his fingers clenched in fists. For a moment, he was transported back in time to an empty country field in Hiroshima, which he and his brothers cleared for their personal baseball diamond. They cut up a soiled tatami mat to make the bases and secured together three short bamboo poles to use as a bat. They wrapped rags to form a lopsided ball. Besides judo, baseball was the sport for them, ever since Babe Ruth had come to Japan for the exhibition games in 1934.

Mas looked around at Lloyd and his crew, who were all standing, too. Their attention, however, was not on the TV screen but on their greenskeeping equipment. Not fans of either team, they just wanted to do their job and go home.

One crew member said he had to go check out the skin in left field.

Lloyd must have seen the puzzled expression on Mas's face.

"That's what we call the grass, Dad."

Mas decided to make his way back to the press box, and as he walked there, his phone rang. He flipped it open.

"*Ojisan*," Yuki said, "we have to go to the hospital immediately."

"Orai. I comin'." Before Mas even said that much, Yuki had clicked off. Something had happened to Jin-Won, Mas figured. First Itai and now the Korean knuckleball pitcher. Was this some kind of Japanese far-right-wing plot?

When he finally met the reporter in the hallway, it was worse than he had initially imagined.

"It's Jin-Won's grandmother," Yuki informed him as they rushed to the Impala. "She collapsed while watching the game."

Did someone purposely harm the old woman? Mas wondered as he got into the driver's seat. His hands shook as he held the steering wheel. They were stuck in the parking lot gridlock, which agitated Yuki no end.

"How did you find out?" Mas asked in Japanese, hoping that conversation would calm Yuki down.

"Amika told me. I knew something was up from the way the Korean media was huddled together."

Forty-five minutes later, they finally arrived at White Memorial Hospital in East Los Angeles, a trip that without the baseball traffic would have taken them fifteen minutes.

Mas braced himself for bad news. That poison, the cyanide, had taken hold of Itai in a matter of minutes. The Korean grandmother was almost twice his age—and most likely had had a broken body for most of her life—so surely she could not survive its effects.

When they walked down the hall toward intensive care, Mas noticed someone leaning against the wall. At first he thought it was a teenage boy, but as they got closer, he could clearly make out the uniform and the black layered hair.

"Neko-*san*." Yuki stood in front of her, opening himself up for any kind of response, even another slap. But there was no slap. Neko literally fell into his arms, pressing her face in his shoulder and shaking with sobs.

Mas felt so awkward; he didn't know if he should stay or go. He stuffed his right hand into his jacket pocket. There was something round in the pocket—the baseball with Japanese writing. He then checked his left: some quarters. He went back toward the elevator to buy the girl a Coke from a vending machine.

When he returned, both young people were sitting on the floor, their backs against the wall. He handed the Coke bottle to Neko, who accepted it appreciatively with a bow of the head. Yuki took it from her and screwed open the cap while she cleaned her face with a handkerchief.

She took a long sip of the Coke. "I can't believe this is happening," she said, her voice wavering. Mas was afraid the girl would start crying again. "Just when I met her."

Mas and Yuki exchanged glances. What was she talking about?

Neko picked up on their confusion. "Don't you know?" Her long eyelashes were clumped from her tears. "Mrs. Kim is my grandmother."

"So Jin-Won…."

"He's my cousin."

"I don't understand." Yuki's voice was gentle and soft. "Mrs. Kim is Korean."

Just when Yuki spoke those words, the realization hit both him and Mas. According to Itai's notes, Mrs. Kim had been a comfort woman. Somehow that connection had led to the birth of a child, either Neko's father or mother.

Neko didn't reply and dabbed her eyes again with her handkerchief. Her nose had become swollen and red. Mas hated to think it, but the girl looked like a mess.

"When did you find out?"

"Jin-Won approached me the first day I arrived here in Los Angeles. The day before the game."

"It must have been a shock."

"The funny thing was, it really wasn't. It was like someone had been preparing for me to finally learn the truth. I grew up with secrets. I knew my father was born in Manchuria; my Japanese grandparents were stuck there during World War II. My grandparents never talked about it. And neither does my father. A taboo topic. That's why I told Amika to tread lightly."

"Amika?" Yuki withdrew from Neko for a moment, as if she could smell his intimate encounter with the TV reporter.

"She insisted on speaking with my parents in Yokohama. Said that it was essential for her profile on me. I'm not sure exactly what she said, but whatever it was, it deeply offended them. They were so upset. Apparently, my father threw the whole news crew out of their house. They were furious with me, too, but wouldn't say why. And they cut off ties with my grandparents. I immediately called Amika to find out what had happened, and she claimed that my parents had overreacted. But to what? I still to this day don't know exactly, but I can guess." Neko took another sip of her soda. "They didn't want to consider that my father had been adopted. And even worse, that he'd been a product of something unspeakable."

Amika knew more than she was letting on to them, Mas thought.

"Mrs. Kim had given birth in Manchuria. A boy. He was taken from her and given up for adoption at an orphanage. For the last five years, Jin-Won has been helping her find out what happened to him."

"Your father."

Neko nodded. "My father. I didn't know he'd been adopted, and I don't think he even knew until Amika told him. Jin-Won took me out to dinner and showed me the paperwork. Given that my grandparents had been so secretive all these years, it made sense. They hadn't done anything wrong; they'd done a good thing, in fact. Gave my father a second chance at life. But why keep it a secret?"

Mas, who had harbored some secrets of his own, understood Neko's grandparents' motivation. What good would it be to dig up dark secrets from the past? Why hoist that dead weight onto your children and grandchildren?

"That's why you were so tender toward Jin-Won. He's your blood," Yuki said it aloud, obviously more for his benefit than Neko's.

She nodded. "You know that I'm an only child. To have

a younger cousin, another knuckleball pitcher, with a baby. And a new grandmother. In one week, my family multiplied." The girl's face darkened again. "But now I might lose my grandmother, just when I met her." Neko began to cry again, and Mas couldn't take it anymore.

He wandered back to the vending machine, but his pocket held no more quarters. He was checking his worn wallet when he felt someone's presence. That woman, Sally Lee, aiming her camera toward him.

Mas frowned. All this photo-taking and spying had to stop. "Whyzu you take my pikucha?"

"I have a better question. Why are you here? You're no friend or relative to Mrs. Kim."

Well, I'm no enemy, either, he thought.

"You don't belong here. The police are on their way anyway. Get out of here before I call security."

Mas was in no mood to make a scene in an intensive care ward, so he stumbled away.

"Letsu go," he said to Yuki, adding in Japanese, "we are not wanted here."

"I'm staying put, *Ojisan*," Yuki said. His arm was around Neko's slumped shoulders. He was back in the pitcher's good graces, and he wasn't going to budge.

Suit yourself, Mas thought. He wasn't going to hang around where he wasn't wanted, to be possibly accused of being a killer, or maybe be killed himself.

★ ★ ★

The first thing Mas wanted to do was drive to Genessee's and sit back on her couch, listening to her plucking her Okinawan banjo-like instrument, the *sanshin*. But that wasn't an option, at least not now. To go back to that meant he'd have to commit to some changes, and he didn't know if he could really follow through.

He got into the Impala and closed the heavy door behind him. Were they dealing with some kind of deranged serial killer? First to be downed was Itai, who seemed somewhat sensitive to the plight of the comfort women, and now a comfort woman herself?

He needed something to help him escape his worries. He'd stopped smoking, and he hardly drank anymore. But a soft bean-and-cheese burrito, easy on the dentures—that would be something to enjoy. There was no parking lot for Al & Bea's, so he had to fight churchgoers (why were the churches around here open almost every night?) and mariachi musicians for an open spot on First Street. The eatery was literally a shack with an aluminum awning and practically no sign. But anyone who was anyone in L.A. knew that they made the best bean-and-cheese burritos.

Mas finally found a spot near the freeway onramp and slowly made his way to the street. It was pitch dark now, with no visible streetlights. The sidewalks were sometimes damaged into concrete crumbles, so Mas knew he needed to take it slow.

Before he reached the curb, two men blocked his path.

"Are you for us or are you against us?" one of them said in English, his accent betraying his Japanese background.

Who was "us"? Mas wondered. The one who spoke looked about forty, and he had a faint mustache.

"*Omae*, do you understand?" the other added forcefully in Japanese. He was chubby in tight pants, which gave the illusion that his middle was melting.

No, Mas thought, *I don't*, but it wasn't a good time to admit that.

"Are you a traitor to Japan?" asked the mustachioed man.

"I'm American," Mas said in Japanese. "So if that makes me a traitor, then I am."

"So you are on the side of the United States. The people who want to take over our land for army bases. To make us toothless. Impotent."

"You drop bombs on us, seeking to obliterate us," the chubby one added.

"*Chotto, chotto*," Mas said. That's one thing he could not let pass. "I'zu a *hibakusha*."

"Atomic-bomb survivor? You? Where were you?"

"At the Hiroshima train station." He gave the exact address and the name of his school.

"I cannot believe this," said the chubby one.

"So you know what they're saying about these 'comfort women' are lies." The mustachioed man was more of a talker. "Those brothels were not sanctioned by the military. They were independent from the Japanese government. Those women volunteered to work there for money."

Mas was too young to have fought for the army, so he had no idea what was going on in different parts of Asia, or even in his own backyard. It was actually Yuki who'd told him about the Koreans who were forcibly brought over by the Imperial Army to work in defense factories in places like Hiroshima.

"I dunno nuttin'," Mas said, changing to English. "I'zu no soldier. But you'zu two plain too young to knowsu either."

The mustachioed man cursed him and spit on the ground in front of Mas.

"You just watch out, old man," the chubby one said. "You don't want to fall down dead like Itai some day."

As they strolled away, the traffic on the nearby freeway buzzed in Mas's ears. He realized that he'd seen these two before. They were the men following the yellow-haired outfielder, Kii Tanji, back at Dodger Stadium.

Chapter Nine

Mas didn't know if the boy journalist would be answering his phone in the hospital, but he tried calling anyway.

He'd just finished polishing off his second bean-and-cheese burrito—he thought he deserved it, after the encounter with the two *hanakuso* good-for-nothings, little bugger snots that Mas could have quickly brushed aside when he was in his prime. But he wasn't in his prime now, and he knew it.

"Mas-*san*, hello." There was a lightness to Yuki's voice, a carefree warmth that Mas had never heard before. It didn't surprise him when Yuki reported that Mrs. Kim's condition had stabilized. Tests revealed no cyanide in her bloodstream, although it was possible that other poisons could be present. Unfortunately, testing for unknown chemicals could take days to process in the laboratory.

Mas told Yuki about the two men and the threat delivered by the roly-poly one. "I saw these two *kuso*-heads with Kii Tanji this morning," Mas said in Japanese. "They were following him around like hungry dogs."

"I think I know who you're talking about. Just a minute, okay?" Mas heard Yuki speak to someone, most likely Neko. "Come pick me up at the hospital. I think we need to have a conversation with Tanji-*san*."

"Maybe police betta handle," Mas said.

"No, they have no idea what's going on," Yuki said. "You need to be from Japan to really understand."

★ ★ ★

When Mas went to the hospital to pick Yuki up, he noticed Sally Lee standing by the glass doors. As soon as he parked the Impala by the entrance, she crossed her arms and scowled, as if to say, *Didn't I tell you to stay away?*

"Whatsu dat lady's problem, anyhowsu?" Mas asked after Yuki got into the car and closed the door.

"Who?" Yuki buckled his seat belt. "Oh, Sally Lee. She's kind of Mrs. Kim's assistant while she's in Los Angeles."

"Sheezu the one who told me to leave."

"She's just trying to protect Mrs. Kim. Don't take it seriously, *Ojisan*. She's actually not bad when you get to know her."

Yah, right, thought Mas. He'd as soon see flowers bloom from a rock before that ever happened.

★ ★ ★

Tanji was staying at the Bonaventure like all the other

Japanese team members. Neko had called him, feigning that she needed to talk to him about a very important matter.

Yuki even had his room number, so he and Mas went into the glass tube-like elevator with a clear mission: find out what Tanji was up to. And make sure to warn him to keep his minions far away from Mrs. Kim, who had to remain at White Memorial Hospital for who knows how many days.

Neko chose to stay with her grandmother in her hospital room. It made sense. She and Jin-Won needed to focus their energies on helping their elder get better. Yuki and Mas, on the other hand, had dirty work to do.

Climbing to the twenty-ninth floor, Mas looked out the elevator's glass walls at the downtown L.A. skyline. It was now close to ten o'clock, yet some floors of the office skyscrapers were still lit up, either for the cleaning crews or late-night workaholics. He felt as though he was lifting off into space, until the glass pod shuddered to a stop. It was time to get out and face Tanji.

Tanji was obviously expecting Neko, so he opened the door immediately after they knocked. "*Ara—*" he said, stepping into the carpeted hallway to see if Neko was lagging behind Mas and Yuki.

Yuki pushed Tanji back into his room. Mas was shocked by the audacity but impressed by this new Yuki, transformed after being reconciled with his true love. "We have some questions for you, Tanji."

"Oh, you do now?" Tanji sneered, revealing crooked teeth. Mas never understood why the young Japanese, even the rich ones, never seemed to fix their teeth. Mas and

Chizuko had spent a small fortune to correct Mari's, and she was no superstar celebrity.

Tanji's room was more expansive than regular hotel rooms, with fancier lighting and furniture. His hair was still wet from the shower, blunting the shock of the blondness.

Sitting on the edge of the king bed, he gestured toward a comfortable chair with a matching ottoman. Yuki took his position on the ottoman and flipped open Itai's computer, which never seemed to leave his side. Mas chose to keep standing.

Tanji took out a cigarette from a pack that he held in his left hand. Mas was surprised to see that it was a brand he recognized from the 1930s. Golden Bat. The cheapest of cheap, and filterless. As Tanji lit his cigarette, Mas almost starting salivating. These young men from Japan would be the death of him. More days of spending time with them, and he'd be back smoking again.

Tanji must have noticed the longing in Mas's eyes, because he held out the pack of Golden Bats to both him and Yuki. Mas hesitated but still shook his head. Once the smoking started, it could not be stopped. Besides, wasn't this hotel nonsmoking like all the other ones? Tanji was a bigwig who obviously considered himself immune to rules. Yuki was still busy trying to find something on the laptop.

"Interesting slogan," said Tanji, smoke coming out of the gaps between his teeth. He gestured toward the sticker—sure enough, he was talking about the characters for *teia,* 帝亜, on the back of the computer.

"You know what that means?" Mas asked in Japanese.

Tanji shook his head. "No idea."

"This is Itai-*san*'s computer," Yuki finally said. "There are some very interesting things on here. Like this." He turned the laptop around, and even Mas was taken aback. On the screen was a photo of Tanji with the same two men who'd confronted Mas in East L.A. "Can you explain this to us? Itai-*san* took it the day before he was killed."

Tanji's face didn't change expression. Mas was looking very carefully for signs. He thought he saw a very brief shadow cast over Tanji's eyes, but the darkness quickly left, like the grayness below fast-moving storm clouds. "What of it? It's just me with two local fools." He'd already finished one cigarette and started on his second. Mas didn't know how these star athletes could compete with so much damage to their lungs.

"Why are you spending so much time with them?"

"I don't see how it's your business."

"They threatened my driver here," Yuki said. "They told him they might kill him if he was sympathetic to the *ianfu* issue."

"*Ianfu*? I don't get it." Tanji, at least to Mas, seemed genuinely perplexed.

"Jin-Won's grandmother is an *ianfu*. She's in the hospital right now, perhaps a result of somebody's dark mischief."

"Well, I'm sorry to hear that. Really, I am. But I had nothing to do with it. Absolutely nothing."

"Then why spend time with these 'fools,' as you call them?"

Good question, Yuki, Mas thought.

Tanji dropped his second cigarette into an empty beer can. "If I tell you, you can't write this, Kimura. At least not now. I'll give you the green light when it's official."

Yuki didn't agree, but he didn't disagree, either. His silence gave tacit approval to Tanji's offer.

"I'm retiring from baseball after this season and going back home to Kagoshima. I plan to run for an open spot in the Lower House."

"I'd heard some rumors," Yuki said. "But how does your political campaign have anything to do with those characters?"

"I'm not hanging out with them, okay? They're from my prefecture. They've been following me around town. I can't chase them away...."

"Because that wouldn't be smart politically."

The blond would-be politician nodded. "I'm worried about the future of Japan. We used to be a world economic and political power. Our automobile industry may soon be overtaken by other Asian countries. What can we offer? The best anime and manga out there? The most gorgeous sushi? There's got to be more."

Both Yuki and Mas remained silent. Tanji had a point.

Tanji continued to address Yuki. "You're young. You know how it is with your friends. All these young men and women unemployed. Lost in a fantasy world with their computers. They're afraid to come out of their rooms. Is this our Japanese future? Trapped on our little island?"

"But surely we can't go back to Imperial Japan? Look how damaging that was to us, the rest of Asia, the world."

"That was the past. We have to look to the future."

"Maybe not making peace with that past is what's keeping us back," Yuki said.

"Now you sound like Itai. He was always crying about what happened sixty, seventy years ago. How does that help us today? It just crushes our spirit. Just look at Zahed. He has no idea who he is, how much talent he has. I try to egg him on, to encourage him to be strong, but he doesn't seem like he can take the pressure."

Mas was surprised to hear Tanji say this. Wasn't he the one who'd said disparaging things about the young man's pitching record in the minors? But then again, that was the traditional way of doing things in Japan. To scold and correct the younger ones, the *kohai*—not because you lorded over them, but because you wanted the best for them.

"Ah—" Mas interrupted. He remembered then that Tanji had approached Itai in the press box dining room on Itai's last living day. Mas had forgotten to tell Yuki; he reported what he'd heard right now.

Yuki's face grew still as he listened to Mas. He turned to Tanji. "What did you two talk about?"

Tanji's jaw tightened, and Mas expected him to repeat *None of your business.* He instead took a deep breath. "He asked to see me. He wanted me to ease up on Zahed. Said that my approach wasn't helping him play better."

"And you said?"

"I refused, of course. I'm not going to let a tabloid journalist tell me what to do on the field."

"And these two guys?" Yuki again flashed the computer

image of the mini-thugs who had bothered Mas. "What are their intentions?"

"They don't have the balls to hurt anyone," Tanji said. "They talk a lot, but when it comes right down to it, a barking dog doesn't bite."

★　★　★

After getting back in the Impala, Mas didn't start the engine right away. He was still a bit shaken by the encounter with the two fools, regardless of whether they really were a legitimate threat. But what was more disconcerting was Yuki's conversation with Tanji. The veteran baseball player was a convincing speaker, but then weren't all politicians? Many were great manipulators of feelings; perhaps Tanji was one of them with this dangerous gift.

"Whatchu think?" he asked Yuki directly.

"When I think about it, it makes sense that Tanji is contemplating a career in politics. He was meeting a lot with various community leaders here in Los Angeles. It wouldn't be the first time that a Japanese politician came to the US to court international support."

Mas fumbled with his keys.

"But on the other hand," Yuki continued, "I think he's hiding something. I don't believe for one moment that Itai-*san* was telling him how to treat Zahed. I think this has something to do with his future as a politician."

Mas gave his passenger a sidelong glance.

"It's all in Itai-*san*'s notes," Yuki said. "He'd actually heard that Tanji was planning to retire from baseball and run for office. Even sent Tanji an email about it. But Tanji denied it. It's all in here." Yuki patted the laptop. "Maybe Itai-*san* was planning to write something about Tanji's candidacy. Along with his connection with these right-wing nuts who traveled to L.A."

Mas didn't know about Japanese politics, but figured campaign dirt was still dirt, no matter what the country. Would that be enough to cause a man to commit murder?

★   ★   ★

After they returned to Little Tokyo, Yuki invited Mas to go out for a late-night snack. Mas tried to defer; he had two bean-and-cheese burritos rolling around his stomach, after all. It was now close to midnight, and the only place open seemed to be Suehiro's, a Japanese diner on the other side of Yuki's hotel on First Street.

Apparently lots of other people—mostly young—had had the same idea, so most of the booths were occupied. There was one empty table for two in the middle of the diner, not very comfortable with its metal chairs, but it would have to do.

After they ordered—Mas opted for simple *ochazuke*, the bowl of green tea over rice he often ate at home—they returned the laminated menus to the side of the napkin dispenser. A party in the far corner exploded in laughter—all twentysomethings whose faces were flushed with drink.

Mas had been thinking more about Itai's protectiveness

toward Zahed. "Youzu know that Itai was buddy-buddy with the boy pitcher?"

Yuki, who was promptly served a bowl of miso soup, nodded. He broke his disposable wood chopsticks in half and stirred the cloudy soup with the ends of his chopsticks. "Yeah, Itai was funny about Zahed. He kind of lost all editorial judgment there. Itai, as far as I knew, didn't have children, but Zahed was like his son."

Mas pictured the middle-aged journalist with his pitiful wilted goatee standing next to the towering, skinny *hapa* pitcher. What a pair they made.

"Maybe it was that Kyoto pride or something. They went to the same high school, you know. At different times, of course. But Itai-*san* still would not advocate on Zahed's behalf. He wouldn't cross that line."

"Zahed tole me that Itai was doin' stories on him since he was in junior high."

A plate of pork *tonkatsu*, cabbage salad, and a mound of rice was placed in front of Yuki. Mas's humble bowl of *ochazuke* looked perfectly peasant-like in comparison.

"I didn't know that," Yuki said in between bites of rice. He squirted dark brown sauce on top of the sliced fried pork cutlet. "But it doesn't surprise me. Itai-*san* always rooted for the underdogs, the minorities. His family, in fact, bounced around between Japan and the US. That's why his cousin, Sunny, lives here. Sunny's brother, on the other hand, died recently in Japan."

Mas took a big slurp of his *ochazuke*. "Oh, yah?"

"Sorry, my phone. It's Neko." Yuki, still chewing,

excused himself and took her call outside.

Mas took out his phone while he was alone at the table. Flipping it open, he was greeted by the current time, 12:38 a.m. He didn't know the last time he'd stayed out so late. There were no voicemail messages waiting. No calls from Genessee. Being that it was after midnight, Mas knew that he shouldn't be calling anyone. But Genessee was a late-night person, who at this hour was often curled up on the corner of her living room couch, a hand-stitched quilt from her paternal grandmother around her slim shoulders. On her stereo system was usually a CD, perhaps folk music from Okinawa, a classical symphony, or even sometimes a rock song. Genessee had many different dimensions to her, dimensions that he ardently missed right now. It was as if eating the *ochazuke* had taken all the sour pretense out of his system. He needed Genessee, really needed her, and before he knew it, he was calling her home number. The telephone rang once, twice, and then her recorded message came on. What? Where was she at this hour? If she was home, she surely would have answered the phone, fearing some kind of emergency. Then the beep to leave a message, and Mas could only breathe into his cheap cell phone once before snapping it closed. Then the table in the corner roared again, and this time Mas silently cursed them for their momentary happiness. *Happiness is indeed fleeting*, he thought. *Before you know it, it's gone forever.*

Chapter Ten

"Y"ou look tired, *Ojisan,*" Yuki said after returning to
the table at Suehiro's.

It's no wonder, thought Mas, *at this hour.*

"Sleep in my room tonight. My bed is big enough."

Mas frowned. *What kind of offer was the boy making?*

"Don't be *baka.* I'm not saying anything untoward. I just
don't want to worry about you driving home in that old car."

Huh! That old car had been safely transporting them
all around town. But Mas didn't have the energy to argue.
Frankly, just thinking about collapsing into a bed with a
fresh set of sheets was too enticing.

The next morning, Mas woke uncertain of where he
was. The plump pillow with its starchy case felt unfamiliar
under his head. And there were no layered smells of the past:
the hint of the Shiseido toner that Chizuko applied on her
face every night before going to bed, the ancient mothballs
from her underwear drawer that he still hadn't cleaned out,
and the medicated Salonpas patches from when his back
gave out a couple of years ago. Instead he smelled nothing,

or at least it seemed like nothing. Maybe a nothing that was trying too hard.

He opened his eyes to a harsh light coming from the large window that faced north. And the sound of tapping buttons. It was Yuki sitting in front of Itai's laptop at the desk at the Miyako Hotel. His hair was frizzled and tangled; Mas's probably wasn't much better. The reporter squinted at the screen through his black plastic glasses. His dedicated concentration made him seem, Mas had to admit, halfway intelligent.

Mas pulled himself up on the firm mattress and rolled to his feet on the padded carpet. After going *shi-shi*, he washed his hands and reluctantly studied his face in the bathroom mirror. With a shadow of black and gray whiskers and bags under his eyes, he definitely looked like shit.

"You have to look at this," Yuki said from his seat at the desk when Mas returned to the main room.

Mas stretched his back until he heard his spine popping, releasing a night's worth of tension. He slowly made his way to the desk.

"I was looking through Itai-*san*'s web browser, and I came across this," Yuki said, turning the laptop toward Mas.

The screen was filled with Japanese words.

"Can't see dat," Mas commented, making a half-hearted effort to search for his glasses.

"I'll read it to you," Yuki said. He began reciting a string of hate, all aimed toward the Koreans and some people called the *Zainichi*.

Sickened, Mas read over Yuki's shoulder. "*Zai-nichi*."

Living in Japan. He had heard that term before but wasn't sure what it exactly meant.

"That means Koreans living in Japan. Goes back to when Korea was under Japanese rule in the 1900s. They came to work—sometimes even forced to work—in Japan during World War II. Afterwards, most went back to Korea, since they didn't have many rights in Japan. Some of the ones who stayed, their children or grandchildren, went on to become citizens, but others continue to live in Japan as permanent residents. It's not like America, where you're automatically a citizen if you're born in the US. To become a Japanese citizen, you have to pretty much erase your cultural background."

Mas had never given much thought to minorities in Japan. When he was there, it seemed like every face was like his. But now with young people like Soji Zahed, Japan was changing, just like in America. And like in America, some people didn't seem happy about it.

"Whozu writin' dat kind of stuff?"

"Well, that's the whole thing. It's anonymous. It's like graffiti you'd find on the walls of a public toilet. We don't know for sure. Maybe some teenagers who are too afraid to deal with the real world. Unemployed men and women. And, of course, the right-wingers who believe that Japan somehow needs to be protected from outsiders."

These were only words, right? Mas thought. *Anyone could say something. It didn't mean that they would actually do something.*

"Anyway, I'm looking at the walls of this web toilet, and

guess what I find?"

Mas was afraid to even think about it.

"A thread on Itai-*san*."

Mas had no idea what Yuki was talking about, so he waited for the boy to elaborate. He resumed reading from the computer screen: "Our liberal enemy has been eliminated. The liar, Tomo Itai, has died in Los Angeles."

Mas couldn't believe what he was hearing. How did these numbskulls know that Itai was dead? As far as he knew, it hadn't been reported in either the local papers or the Japanese ones. Itai did write about famous people, but that didn't mean that he was famous himself.

"This lover of the Korean and *Zainichi* fell to his death at a baseball stadium in Los Angeles. His face covered in vomit."

Mas's jaw grew slack. *How the hell did this writer know such details? He could only have known because he was there.*

"And that's not all. Someone else wrote, 'Cyanide poisoning is the proper demise for someone who poisons Japan.' It's dated Friday, 7 p.m., Pacific time."

"That's about the time we found how Itai was killed," Mas said in Japanese.

Yuki nodded. "It has to be someone who's here in Los Angeles, who's either reporting on the baseball games or...."

Mas could finish the sentence in his mind. *Or killed him.*

Someone pounded on the door and Mas practically jumped. Yuki cautiously rose from his seat and approached the door.

He looked through the peephole and cringed.

"Let me in, Yuki. I know you're in there." Amika spoke in her native Japanese. "I'm not going to leave until you let me in."

Yuki sighed and opened the door.

Amika walked in, wearing black slacks and a filmy white blouse that tied in a bow around her neck. She looked sweet, almost like a gift, until she opened her mouth. "Were you the one telling the police that I had it out for Itai?"

"I didn't say a word."

She pulled out a swivel chair by the desk and planted herself in it, crossing her legs like she meant business. "Look, I did hate Itai, because he's a story-stealing weasel." Mas wondered how that was going to prove her innocence. "But I didn't want him to die. The police couldn't figure out how I could have obtained cyanide, so they had to let me go. I had to account for every minute that I've been here. They've been interviewing all my colleagues. Even the cameraman! I told them that they're barking up the wrong tree. Wasting precious investigative time. And they don't have anything. Now they're talking about suicide."

"Suicide?" Now Yuki was interested in what Amika was saying. "Itai-*san* would be the last person who would commit suicide."

"I know that. You know that. But I think these American detectives have been watching *Shogun* or too many samurai movies. I'm surprised that they haven't spoken to you yet."

"I did talk with them at Dodger Stadium. But I didn't

mention you. They wanted to know if Itai-*san* had enemies. Too many to name, I told them. Just read his past articles. But then, of course, they can't. It's all in Japanese."

"I thought they had an Asian task force or something. You know, from back in the days of the Miura incident." Amika registered Yuki's blank look. "You know about the Miura incident, right?"

"Of course," Yuki said, not so definitively.

"Don't lie. Oh my gosh."

Even Mas knew about the Miura incident. Anyone who had been around in L.A. in the 1980s did. A Japanese businessman, Miura, and his wife were shot in a robbery in a parking lot not far from the Bonaventure Hotel, and she died. Los Angeles was dangerous, full of unsavory minorities—that was the message that the anguished, wounded husband had told the newspapers, both here and in Japan. As it turned out, Miura had planned the whole thing to collect a handsome insurance settlement. He'd been able to evade American prosecution for decades, until recently.

"He killed himself in jail here in L.A. last year," Yuki spouted out, the gears in his brain finally working. "He wrote on his blog that he was going to Saipan from Japan, and the American authorities caught him there." He exhaled as if he'd achieved a physical feat.

"Not bad, not bad." Amika pulled a piece of lint off of her skirt.

"Why are you really here? It's not only to test me about crimes committed before I was born."

"I want to know how Mrs. Kim is doing. Jin-Won won't

answer my calls."

"Probably because you're on Neko's blacklist."

Amika's face fell slightly, but she quickly lifted her chin as if she was lifting her spirits. "Why? I haven't done anything against her. And what does Neko have to do with Jin-Won, anyway?" she asked coyly.

Don't you know? Mas thought.

Yuki hesitated, too. "Just that the word gets around to the players and coaches."

"You should talk. The media pool doesn't think much of you, I can tell you that."

Yuki's eyes flashed, and Mas felt bad for the boy.

"I know that *Nippon Series* didn't really send you here. That you bothered them for press credentials, but they refused to pay your expenses. This little trip is all self-financed on your credit card, and you're almost maxed out."

Yuki lowered his head. Then it must be true. No wonder the boy had called on Mas to drive and translate. It wasn't a matter of trust, but a matter of cash. Come to think of it, he'd yet to see a dime for his work.

He had to give the boy credit, however. He continued to stand his ground. "Being a freelancer is legitimate," he said.

"Yeah, keep telling yourself that." Amika recrossed her legs. "So, anyway, how is Mrs. Kim doing? I saw you two walking into the hospital."

"What, have you been following me? And after these insults, you think that I'll even answer?"

"Listen, grow up. We're both adults. If you want to be a

real reporter, act like one. You share some information with me, and I'll give you a lead."

"What possible lead could I get from you?"

"I'll share if you do."

Don't do it, Mas said to himself. But Amika was too powerful a force.

"They found no sign of cyanide in her system, okay? She's holding steady."

"Thank you."

Yuki crossed his arms. "Okay, so what's your lead?"

"Do you want to write this down?"

Yuki tapped his head. "I can remember."

Amika shrugged her shoulders and began: "Before he left for Los Angeles, Itai met with the baseball commissioner in Tokyo. Had some secret meetings."

"About what?"

"I'm not sure, but the commissioner was very upset. Knowing Itai, he probably came up with some dirt about the league."

"That's it?"

"Well, if I knew more, I would have reported it already."

"Hmmm. There was that lost *Gurippu* document," Yuki murmured, more to himself than to anyone else.

"What's that?"

"Ah, nothing." Yuki picked up his phone from the desk. "Sorry, but we have a morning appointment."

Amika crinkled her nose. She didn't seem to believe Yuki but reluctantly moved toward the door. She still wanted to have the last word. "Listen, we can help each other out, you know. Like this."

"Yes, yes." Yuki pushed his glasses atop his head as if he didn't want to see her anymore.

Once the heavy hotel door had closed, Mas held out his hands. "Well?"

"It's hard to know if I can trust her."

"Why youzu tell her about Missus Kim?"

"So she'd leave her alone. And stop following us. As long as she doesn't think there's a story, we'll be okay."

"Why youzu enemies, anyhowsu?"

"I wouldn't say enemies, per se." Yuki hesitated for a moment. "Well, to be perfectly honest, Itai-*san* probably did wrong her."

"What youzu mean?"

"Based on what Neko has said, Amika was the one who found out that Mrs. Kim was an *ianfu*. But for some reason, she hasn't reported it. Her employer is more conservative. They don't typically cover stories like that."

"Thatsu not Itai's problem."

"True, but I think he did steal the story from her. He's drinking buddies with one of the cameramen who works on her show. I was actually with them at a bar back in Tokyo, and the cameraman mentioned that he'd finished a shoot with Amika and Neko's parents in Yokohama. He probably told Itai what happened. And from there, Itai must have appropriated the information as his own."

Mas knew what it was like to have your customers stolen right from under your nose. No wonder Amika had an axe to grind against Itai and *Nippon Series*.

Mas wanted to cleanse himself of the dirtiness that he'd just heard. "I take shower," he announced.

Yuki gestured toward a bag from their shopping expedition in Little Tokyo the other day. "Go ahead. Feel free to wear what you need."

Inside was a package with white Jockey underwear and a couple of T-shirts. One shirt had a heart over a skeleton, while the other was a Dodgers one with the latest Japanese import, Kuroda, on the back. Mas chose Kuroda, who'd been a former player with the Hiroshima Carp.

Once under the spray of the showerhead, Mas thought about baseball in America, with its string of scandals and controversies. Mas had been among those who swore off baseball for a season in 1995 after the millionaire players returned from going on strike. Wasn't baseball about the fans? Didn't these *senshu* realize that without the fans, there'd be no outlandish salaries in the first place?

And the steroid use. Those stories nearly destroyed the enthusiasm of Tug and his son, who religiously followed the stats. With the effects of these performance-enhancing drugs, did records mean anything anymore? But baseball in that sense were like the *hibakusha*. They rose from the ashes and survived, just like Mas. Were such scandals present in Japanese baseball as well?

When he finally emerged from the steamy bathroom wearing the Dodgers T-shirt, Yuki was back at the desk and the computer. "I wasn't able to recover any files on the laptop," he said without averting his gaze from the screen. "But remember the thumb drive Sunny gave me? There was a file there, too. Not '*Gurippu*' but '*Gurippusuhomu.*'"

Mas repeated the word a couple of times. It was obviously in *katakana*, an alphabet used mainly to phoneticize non-Japanese words.

"It's Gripsholm, I think," Yuki said. "There's a castle in Sweden named Gripsholm. I can't open the file—it's been deleted."

Mas had heard of Gripsholm before. Someone in his circle had mentioned it. Someone at Tanaka's Lawnmower Shop, back before it had been turned into a beauty shop and now exclusively a nail salon. Mas imagined Tanaka's interior. The plain wood shelves full of bags of fertilizer and pesticides. The metal revolving stand of seeds. The one who'd mentioned Gripsholm hadn't been the proprietor, Wishbone Tanaka, but someone close to him: Stinky Yoshimoto, a fellow gardener in Pasadena who'd unfortunately been diagnosed with Alzheimer's last year. Before the diagnosis, Stinky often didn't make much sense, so this new development probably made communication even more difficult. Mas had yet to visit him in the nursing home in Lincoln Heights, but the reports had not been good.

"I may know someone who knows about this Gripsholm," Mas said in Japanese to Yuki. "But he's not hundred percent."

A line formed at the bridge of Yuki's nose. Not a ringing endorsement of a reliable source, that's for sure. He shook away talk about the Gripsholm and went onto a more definite matter. He clicked the keyboard to reveal a website all in Japanese. "Those two good-for-nothings that threatened you in East L.A.—they aren't strangers to Tanji. They're distant relatives named Tanji, too." Scrolling down the page, he stopped on a photo of the men posing with Kii Tanji at Dodger Stadium. "I found them on a blog based in Kagoshima. It has their whole itinerary. And they haven't left Los Angeles yet. This afternoon they'll be at a luncheon organized by a Kagoshima prefectural organization. In a place called Quiet Cannon in Montebello. Have you heard of it?"

Mas nodded. Practically every gardeners' event was held at Quiet Cannon, next to the Montebello Golf Course. If those Tanjis were out to make trouble, they'd chosen the wrong place.

"Letsu go," Mas said.

Chapter Eleven

Montebello used to be a flower town; it even had a generic flower featured on banners drooping from light poles on its main streets. Haruo's second wife, Spoon, had lived there for some time, and when the two aging lovebirds got hitched, Haruo abandoned his postage-stamp apartment in the Crenshaw district in central L.A. to move in with her and her adult daughter, Dee. It had been rough going at first, but now they'd become a finely tuned household. The three of them had a special-event floral business, and they'd turned the garage into a makeshift shed with long tables for young mothers and high school students to thread leis and braid ti leaves for graduations and parties.

Quiet Cannon was on the far north side of town, butted up against the 60 Freeway. Mas had no idea why it was called Quiet Cannon, as the drone of the freeway was anything but quiet, and there was nothing remotely military about the place. But as you turned the corner into the event center, past an *agua* store, a tattoo parlor, and mom-and-pop eateries, the neighboring eighteen-hole city golf course and the towering line of pine and eucalyptus did deafen the urban din. The facility was the go-to place for many a Japanese American event, especially *shinnenkai*, New Year's installation luncheons, as well as weddings and quinceañeras serving the locally dominant Latino community.

In fact, this afternoon, as Mas drove the Impala up the wide bend toward the parking lot, he spotted a team of dark-haired fifteen-year-old girls, teetering in high heels and holding up their long, poofy dresses as they walked past old Japanese couples in dark clothing and sensible shoes.

He and Yuki did not have formal invitations to the Kagoshima prefectural party, which could prove to be a problem. At every event here, the *uketsuke*, or receptionists, sat at a long table at the front doorway, their eagle eyes fixated on a pile of RSVP cards or a typed guest list. A large box on the side held boutonnieres, usually carnations, for the male VIPs and corsages, usually orchids, for the women. Every guest received an adhesive nametag as well a drink ticket and table assignment. Neither Mas nor Yuki would have any of these. Their clothing also wouldn't help them blend in. Mas was in the Dodgers Kuroda T-shirt, while Yuki wore the skeleton one with a heart and the message, "Love Kills."

"Ready?" Yuki asked Mas, after the Impala was parked.

Mas grunted. He hoped he wouldn't run into anyone he knew, but, of course, after they climbed up the stairs to the second-floor banquet room, he saw a familiar face.

"Arai-*san*, long time no see." It was one of the leaders of the gardeners' federation, Kengo Toda, dressed in the customary ill-fitted suit and old-fashioned tie. He was about twenty years younger than Mas, but his wavy hair and mustache already had plenty of gray. Luckily, Toda was speaking mostly in English; the Kagoshima dialect of Japanese sometimes seemed like another language to Mas.

"But you Hiroshima, *desho*?" Toda remarked. "Not Kagoshima."

"Dis my friend," Mas said. "Yukikazu Kimura. Reporter with *Nippon Series*. Heezu visitin' from Kagoshima."

Yuki's mouth dropped open to hear Mas identify him as a Kagoshiman rather than a Hiroshima boy. Some called Kagoshima the Hawaii of Japan. Yuki knew little of either Kagoshima or Hawaii. He quickly recovered and bowed respectfully toward Toda. "*Dozo yoroshiku.*"

"Weezu don't have tickets to dis thing," Mas informed his friend.

"No *shinpai*. I got you covered. A couple called in sick at our table."

And just like that, the doors of hospitality magically opened for Mas and Yuki, all due to the gardeners' connection.

As Toda went to the receptionist's table to get some handwritten nametags and tickets, Yuki saddled up to Mas. "What if they start asking me things about Kagoshima?"

"Do what you do best," Mas hissed back in Japanese. "Lie."

Yuki inhaled and let out air from his puffed cheeks. *We'll see what the boy is truly made of*, Mas thought.

They received their table assignment, No. 5, and found

themselves seated between Toda and his wife. Offering to fetch their complimentary drinks at the bar, Toda collected their red tickets and asked for their orders.

"*Hai-boru*," Yuki said, catching Mas off guard. A highball in the afternoon?

"Coke," Mas said. At least one of them needed to stay sober.

Yuki scanned the room after Toda left. "I don't see Tanji."

Mas grunted. He also hadn't spotted the baseball *senshu* and his bootlickers.

Mas leafed through a glossy bilingual pamphlet left on each seat. It described the history of the Southern California Kagoshima Kenjinkai, a prefectural group started in Los Angeles in 1905. Every Japanese was familiar with Kagoshima's stature as the home of the Satsuma samurai, macho men who held onto their fighting swords until the bitter end.

Servers distributed salads made with iceberg lettuce and grated carrots. Mas was in the middle of passing a salad dressing boat when he noticed that the room of a hundred people had grown hushed. Tanji had entered the banquet hall, the two mini-Tanjis following closely behind. Tanji wore the Japanese formal uniform of a black suit and black tie. He definitely looked the part of a politician.

A man at table 2 stood up and started madly clapping, and one by one, like weeds, they rose, welcoming the celebrity Kagoshiman to their humble event. Tanji was obviously lapping up the attention like fresh milk to an alley cat and began to circle the room. He smiled, revealing his mess of teeth—that is, until he saw Mas and Yuki at table 5. Then he abruptly stopped, causing the entourage behind him to crash into each other.

"Tanji-*san, banzai*!" Again, the man at table 2 expressed his exuberance for the Yomiuri Giants veteran.

Soon, everyone in the room was holding up their wet glasses and toasting Tanji. A few called out the more appropriate and less warlike cheer of *kanpai*, but *banzai* seemed to rule the day.

The Tanjis finally took their places at table 1, allowing the room to settle down and concentrate on the rolls and salad. Toda introduced his wife, an attractive Japanese woman with short chestnut hair who was seated next to Yuki.

"So where in Kagoshima are you from?" she asked in Japanese. Her accent was thankfully not as strong as her husband's.

"Ah, Kagoshima City," Yuki offered up, almost like a question.

Quick thinking, Mas thought disparagingly.

"Oh, I'm from Kagoshima City, too. What part?"

"Ah, well…the east," Yuki said.

"I'm from the east, too. Taniyama. How about you?"

"Further east."

"Further east? Then you'd be in the ocean."

"Well, my family moved to Hiroshima when I was just a baby."

"Oh." The whole table of Kagoshimans seemed disappointed, as if Yuki was a fraud. Which was appropriate, because he was.

Toda, who was at Mas's left, stayed quiet as he buttered his roll. His spirits seemed to rebound after his second gin and soda. "You know that I fought in the Vietnam War, Masao-*san*?"

Mas shook his head.

"My dad came over as a *nanmin*. You know what a *nanmin*, is?" Toda directed his question to Yuki.

"Refugee?"

"There was a refugee act here in America in the 1950s. Japanese barely qualified; we'd suffered through a lot of typhoons, and some Nisei leaders fought to have natural disasters included. My dad got in, just under the gun. Worked on a grape farm. He met my mother in California, they had me and my brothers, and then we went back to Japan."

Mas nodded. It was not an exact echo of his own early life, but similar enough.

"Then when I returned to America—boom, I got drafted. Went from the US back to Asia, only with a machine gun and hand grenades. Half the time I had to avoid getting shot by my own platoon. Needed a sign: I am not the enemy."

Yuki's eyes got as big as quarters, and Mas was reminded how naïve the boy really was. Mas knew that Tug, the American with the Japanese face, fought in high mountain ranges in France, risking his life to save a battalion of soldiers from Texas, while his family and then-girlfriend, Lil, were kicked out of their homes and forced to live in a camp thousands of miles away. If that wasn't irony, Mas didn't know what was.

The emcee, the enthusiastic *banzai* man from table

2, took his place on stage at the podium. He spoke of the proud tradition of Kagoshima, how its geographic isolation in the southern part of Japan had led to fierce independence, yet also ties with foreign countries. He was obviously giddy to be in the presence of Kii Tanji. Mas was starting to feel sick, but not sick enough to refuse the plate of prime rib set in front of him.

The emcee then proceeded to introduce the special guests. He went around the room, almost calling out the name of every person at every table. Finally he got to table 5.

"Kimura Yukikazu," the emcee read from his list of names.

Toda rose to provide additional details. "He's a journalist born in Kagoshima. With *Nippon Series* magazine."

"And your other guest...."

"Ah, Arai Masao."

Toda didn't bother further identifying him, because what could he say? A fellow gardener, with currently only one customer. A has-been. Washed up. Poorer than dirt, with a few coins in his personal bank, a Yuban coffee can in the back of his closet. No, there wasn't much that could be said about Mas Arai, but Mas really didn't care.

There was then a bit of a rumbling at table 1.

The chubby Tanji was on his feet, pointing at Yuki. "He's a liar! He's not from Kagoshima!"

Toda frowned. Sitting back down, he asked Mas for clarification. "You said...."

A skinny man who Mas hadn't seen before stood up and joined the two other Tanjis in casting aspersions on Yuki's credentials.

Yuki's face was as white as that of a ghost. He pointed at his cell phone. "That bony *kuso*-head," he said, pointing to the skinny man with the Tanjis. "He sold me this phone."

"Where? At the tourist office?" Mas asked.

"No, in the hotel parking lot."

The boy had purchased something from someone in a parking lot? Mas had once bought a bowling ball bag from a stranger's trunk outside of his local lanes. As soon as he inserted his fifteen pounder in the bag, the handle fell off.

"I'm on a budget," Yuki said, defending his purchase. "He sold it to me for thirty dollars."

Mas couldn't believe it. *Is that how the Tanji gang seemed to mysteriously know their every move?*

"Damn you!" Yuki shouted at the skinny offender. "You've been spying on me with that piece-of-shit phone you sold me!" He charged toward the table of Tanjis.

Mas bowed his head. "*Moshi wake gozaimasen*," he said to apologize to Toda, who probably needed a third drink.

The skinny Tanji supporter had taken off running, and now he was flying down the stairs toward the golf course, with Yuki at his heels. Behind him were the two Tanjis who had confronted Mas, the chubby one surprisingly leading the other. Bringing up the rear was Kii Tanji, but not for long. Being the true athlete of the bunch, in spite of his smoking habit, he quickly passed the two in the back. Led by the stick-figure man, they zigzagged across the putting green and jumped over parked golf carts. Finally taking a flying leap, Tanji grabbed hold of Yuki's legs, sending him skidding on the green inches away from the eighteenth hole.

"Fore!" High-pitched voices called out, and a neon pink golf ball bounced about two feet from the red flag stuck in the hole.

Mas, who'd been watching all this from the second-floor balcony, spied a group of angry Asian women in visors marching toward the pile of men on the green. You can get away with a lot of things in this world, but not messing with golfers on the eighteenth hole.

By the time Mas made it downstairs, the men, including the skinny one who'd run away in the first place, had wisely moved to the concrete in front of the golf cart check-in area.

"He sold me a tracker phone," Yuki yelled at Tanji. "Your relatives—and yes, we know they're all your relatives," Yuki said, drawing a straight line in the air with his index finger, connecting all the Tanjis on their nametags. "Your relatives have been following us, badgering us. All to protect you. Because you killed Itai-*san*."

Tanji rubbed his yellow crown of hair, which obviously had a generous amount of hair product, because it barely moved. The carnation in his boutonniere was smashed, its stem broken, so the flower hung like a bloody appendage. His face changed expressions quickly—first indignation, then disbelief. He doubled over, but although his face was hidden, the sounds of laughter were unmistakable. "Don't even say a joke like that, Kimura. You're going to kill me with your nonsense."

"It's not nonsense. And it's not a joke. You were seen

before Itai-*san* was killed in the cafeteria, angry about some-thing. Later, he keels over dead, a situation that was cele-brated by your minions on the internet." Yuki sneered at the other Tanjis. "And I've copied everything, so don't even bother trying to erase them from your news boards."

Kii Tanji's muscular body straightened. "Are you seri-ous?" He turned to the mini-Tanjis. "You assholes have been posting things on the internet?"

"It's all anonymous. We didn't use our names or any-thing," the mustachioed one finally said.

"If this miserable, no-good, so-called reporter figured it out, don't you think my political opponents will, too? And it's not like you can get rid of your digital footprint." Tanji started slapping the heads of his minions, who had no choice but to accept their punishment. After a few seconds of that, Tanji stopped and faced Yuki. "Listen, I had noth-ing to do with Itai's death, okay? And they didn't, either. Like I told you before, they're all talk."

"Then why did you confront Itai-*san* on the day he was killed? And don't tell me it had anything to do with Zahed."

Tanji's chest heaved in and out in his formal suit. "He left a message on my phone. That he had some informa-tion that might affect me breaking the home-run record this year."

Yuki didn't seem convinced.

"I didn't tell you because I wasn't sure what he was talk-ing about. Here, listen for yourself." Tanji pulled his phone from his pocket and put it on speaker. A couple of swipes of his screen, and then they heard the familiar raspy voice that

Mas had heard on the Dodger Stadium field: "Tanji, it's Itai. I need to talk to you rght away. It's of the utmost importance. Your future Japan home-run record is on the line."

Tanji returned the phone to his pocket. "So if you got that kind of message, how would you react?"

"What did he say when he spoke to you?" asked Yuki.

"We made arrangements to talk after the game. I have no idea what he was talking about, okay? And why would I want to kill him? If I murdered every journalist who was causing me problems, there wouldn't be hardly anyone in the press corps, okay?"

That actually sounded like it had a ring of truth, Mas thought. Yuki seemed to think the same way. He took a deep breath. "Okay, you *kuso*-heads, you stay away from me and my people. And that includes Neko and Mrs. Kim. You come within ten feet of them and I'll have you arrested, or I'll write something in the *Nippon Series*."

"You don't have to worry," said Tanji. "I have to be back in Tokyo. We're on a plane out of here in two days."

Yuki immediately relaxed. But Mas didn't receive the news of their exit in the same way. The scattering of the Japanese team meant that whoever killed Tomo Itai could conceivably get off scot-free.

★ ★ ★

That evening, Mas and Yuki ended up again at Suehiro's in Little Tokyo. They were seated in the same place with another group of loud youngsters in the place of the ones from the previous night.

"I don't think Tanji killed Itai-*san*," Yuki said after his first chew of his broiled mackerel.

Mas had just dug his fork into his chicken *oyakodonburi*.

"I mean, Itai-*san*'s phone message did sound ominous. But that's it—why would he share Itai-*san*'s phone message with us?"

"You'zu makin' it tough for him."

"Yes, but still. He could have made up another lie." Yuki's phone began ringing, and he excused himself to take the call outside, where it was quieter.

Mas lifted his forkful of chicken, cooked egg, and rice toward his mouth. Chizuko had occasionally made *oyakodonburi* at home. Literally meaning "parent and child bowl," the name was a bit cannibalistic, which added to its charm. But it was really just simple comfort food: a stew of the child (an egg) and the parent (cut-up chicken), with a sauce that combined soy sauce, sugar, and mirin, a low-alcohol rice wine. Genessee made wonderful macaroni and cheese and Greek salad, but *oyakodonburi* wasn't part of her culinary fare.

Yuki returned to the table. "They're going to be moving Mrs. Kim tomorrow from the hospital into a nursing home in Koreatown. Her heart's doing fine, but it turns out that she fractured her hip when she fell. She'll be staying in Los Angeles until she fully recovers."

They decided that Yuki would stay with Neko the next day during the transfer. Mas, on the other hand, had his line of questioning to pursue. One involving a man named Stinky.

Chapter Twelve

Mas had first met Stinky Yoshimoto at Tanaka's Lawnmower Shop in Altadena, near a supermarket called Market Basket. More than for selling equipment and parts, it was most known among gardeners for its covert activities in its backroom. In a haze of cigarette smoke, and around the poker table littered with red pistachio shells, the men traded money and gossip, with the quieter ones typically winning the whole pot at the end of the night. Stinky usually lost.

Mas never knew how Stinky had earned his nickname, and he never wanted to ask. Wishbone Tanaka, the proprietor of the lawnmower shop, was a more formidable figure who usually overshadowed Stinky's ridiculousness. But when you least expected it, Stinky would be inserting his opinion whether you wanted to hear it or not.

Tanaka's was gone, replaced by a nail salon, with its tinny chemical smell instead of the earthy cling of the lawnmower shop. Both Wishbone and Stinky had found refuge at a nursery underneath power lines near Eaton Canyon.

Mas hadn't seen Wishbone's pockmarked mug for a while; he blamed that on the fact that his regular schedule had been upended to accommodate the new additions to his household. Not to mention his friendship with Genessee.

A call to Eaton's Nursery resulted in shocking news. Wishbone had just undergone surgery for stomach cancer. And, coincidentally, he was recovering at the same nursing home in Lincoln Heights where Stinky was now living. The dismal duo, inseparable again.

After Mas got off his cell phone, he felt sadder than hell. It wasn't like he was buddy-buddy with either one of those guys, but he preferred to imagine them causing trouble in multiple neighborhoods rather than rotting away in an institutional box.

He called the nursing home for Wishbone. Would it even be worth talking to Stinky?

"Come on over, Mas," Wishbone said. "Stinky has his good days. He has his bad, too. Either way, it would be good to see you."

Wishbone hadn't been joking about his anticipation. As soon as Mas parked in the lot for the Japanese nursing home on top of the hill in Lincoln Heights, he saw a familiar pigeon-toed man leaning by the front entrance. He had a walker and his back was bent, but sure enough, the old attitude remained. "Hell of a place to see you in, Mas. Here I am, with half a gut. Probably from eating too many *umeboshi*."

Could too many pickled plums kill a man? Mas wondered.

"Just started walking yesterday. Figure that I'll break

out tomorrow."

"Sorry, Wishbone. *Gomen ne.*"

Wishbone scowled. "Nah, not like you had anything to do with it. Getting old is a bitch. But you know that, Mas." His eyes were milky and moist. Mas wondered how long the old man had. "So, what do you want with Stinky? You know that his brain isn't working right. Locked up in the Alzheimer's ward."

Hearing Wishbone say "break out" and "locked up" made Mas want to run in the opposite direction. But he was here to investigate a lead. Find out about the *Gripsholm*. He might as well test it out on Wishbone, Stinky's supposed best friend. "Hey, youzu knowsu about *Gripsholm*?"

"*Gripsholm*? Haven't heard that in long time." Wishbone turned his head awkwardly toward Mas, as if he had a kink in his neck. Mas helped him sit down on a bench.

"Yeah, the *Gripsholm*, that's a story in itself," Wishbone continued. He was wearing a hospital gown and red socks with webbed soles. "It was a fancy Swedish cruise liner at one time, I believe. But during World War II, it went to the dark side and took prisoners of war to Japan from the US. The thing is, they went the long way."

"Whatchu mean, long way?"

"Well, they couldn't just cross the Pacific, right, with all the fighting there. So they went from New York City down to Latin America, South Africa, India, Singapore, the Philippines, and finally Japan."

"Stinky was on it?"

"Stinky? Nah. He's never been east of Las Vegas. Come

to think of it, me neither, if it weren't for camp. Got to see the Bighorn Mountains, compliments of the US government." Wishbone, still full of his piss of sarcasm, puckered his mouth. Maybe his days weren't that numbered after all. "But Stinky was in Tule Lake after his parents went No-No. On the loyalty oath."

Mas struggled to follow what Wishbone was saying. Since Mas had been in Hiroshima during World War II, the goings-on in the camps were a bit of a mystery to him. He'd heard that Tule Lake, right on the California and Oregon border, had the most complicated history. Halfway through its existence, Tule Lake became a segregation center for the No-Nos, folks who wouldn't agree to forswear allegiance to the emperor and fight for America—mostly because they were ridiculous questions, and also because citizenship wasn't even on the table for people straight from Japan. To be a person without any country was a scary proposition, one that Mas knew too well.

"Stinky's old man was one of those types who wasn't going to go down without a fight. You know they were one of the biggest grape growers out by Fresno, right? His dad was so mad about the government telling him that he had to give it all up, that he actually burnt the whole vineyard down to the ground."

Mas completely understood Mr. Yoshimoto's point of view.

"So when they started passing around that questionnaire, Stinky's old man wrote down 'no, no.' Stinky was only sixteen, but he had to go along with what his father wanted, you know."

"He talksu one time about the *Gripsholm. Mukashi, mukashi.*"

"He might have had a girlfriend who was on it or something. That *Gripsholm* all happened before Tule Lake started having a special section for No-Nos. When folks think of *Gripsholm*, they think traitors who rejected America. Wrong-headed, but that's how people are."

Mas felt a bit dejected. It might have been a mistake for him to have come.

Wishbone sensed his disappointment. "Never know what will jog his memory. Can't hurt, at least." Wishbone pushed his walker to the glass door and waited for Mas. "C'mon, I can vouch for you."

Mas wondered about an outfit that would value an endorsement from Wishbone Tanaka. But it didn't matter. All he needed was a way in.

He signed his name on a check-in sheet and followed Wishbone down a hall. The nurse accompanied them to open the door; the Alzheimer's ward was locked for the benefit of the patients who had a penchant for wandering.

Stinky wasn't in his room, which was decorated with hand-drawn pictures from his grandchildren in Seattle. According to Wishbone, Stinky's wife, Bette, was up there now for a quick respite. "She's all skin and bones now," Wishbone said. Mas was surprised to hear about her physical transformation. She was one of those Nisei women who were built sturdy, like a fire hydrant. The fact that she'd lost weight likely meant that caregiving had taken its toll on her.

Mas followed Wishbone from the empty room to an activity center with a large-screen TV and overstuffed couches. A few folding tables were set up, and at one of them, a woman was pushing around puzzle pieces but failing to make any connections. Stinky was in front of the TV, transfixed by the infinite loop of the Japanese cable programming.

"Hey, Stinky. It's Wishbone."

Stinky didn't respond to his lifelong friend's voice. He blinked hard, as if blinking would make the speaker disappear.

Stinky used to have a few long strands of hair that he whipped over his bald scalp like a piece of limp seaweed over a polished rock. Now those sad strands were all gone. Stinky was completely bald, with a pale, green-gray tint to his skin, which made him look like something from outer space. Gardeners weren't meant to be trapped inside, and Stinky was living proof of that.

"This is Mas. You remember Mas Arai, right? Used to garden out our way." Wishbone leaned forward in his walker.

Stinky squeezed his eyes shut and then opened them wide. "Oh, yah, Mas. You have a daughter, right. Jill?"

"No, sheezu Mari," Mas corrected, but Wishbone jabbed him in the ribs to tell him such details were not germane.

"Mas came all this way to ask you a question." Wishbone turned to Mas. "You didn't bring him any chocolates or something, did you? He usually does better with some kind of bribe."

Mas felt embarrassed. Any Japanese worth his salt knows that you bring an *omiyage*, a token gift, when you visit someone. He stuck his hand in his jacket pocket. The baseball that he'd found at Dodger Stadium. He knew it was ridiculous, but he held it out in his palm.

"Baseball! I love baseball," Stinky said, almost squealing. "I played in camp, you know."

"What camp Stinky in?" Mas asked Wishbone.

"Gila River. That's where a lot of those Fresno people went. Pasadena, too."

Sunny Hirose had said that he was in Gila River, Mas remembered. Sunny and Stinky must have been around the same age.

"You knowsu anyone name Itai, no, Hirose?"

"*Itai. Itai.*" Stinky made a sour face and grabbed hold of his calf.

"He banged his leg on the side of his bed," explained Wishbone. "He thinks you're saying the Japanese *itai*."

"No, no." Mas shook his head and tried again. "Sunny Hirose. You knowsu a guy named Hirose?"

"I played shortstop. Made a double play. Won the game. Whee!"

"Stinky, hey, you remember a guy named Sunny Hirose?" Wishbone tried to help, but it was fruitless.

"We beat those yes, yes. Beat those Zenimuras," Stinky said.

"Yah, yah," Mas repeated. Stinky wasn't making any sense at all.

"I thought you were going to ask him about the *Gripsholm*," Wishbone hissed in Mas's ear.

Mas nodded. "You knowsu about *Gripsholm*? I hear

youzu talk about it at lawnmower shop."

"*Gurippusuhomu,*" Stinky repeated. "*Gripsholm.*"

"It's a ship, remember, Stinky? Took *Nihonjin,* including Nisei, to Japan during the war. Didn't you have some girlfriend on that ship?"

"Kawaisoo." Stinky's face got drawn out like a clown's. "She died in the Philippines. So sad."

"They made a stop in the Philippines, I think," Wishbone explained. "Didn't they get transferred onto a second ship?"

Stinky didn't respond. He readjusted his attention back to the television program, a cooking show that was discussing the merits of *natto,* fermented soy beans.

Something vibrated in Wishbone's pocket, and he pulled out his cell phone. It wasn't a clamshell like Mas's, but a top-of-the-line smartphone.

He glanced at the screen. "I gotta get going. My son's here."

"Well, thanks so much, *ne.*"

"I didn't do nothing. If only this guy's head was on straight." Wishbone let out a sigh and tottered away in his walker.

"*Kiyotsuke.*" Mas's last words to Wishbone were to take care. No matter their rocky relationship in the past, they were now bound together with a common destination, with Wishbone likely to be the first one there.

"Yeah, what more can we do, huh?" Wishbone then grinned, his face dissolving into a fan of wrinkles.

Mas decided to stay a little while longer in the

Alzheimer's ward. It began to smell a little like *shikko* in the room, and Mas wondered if someone might have peed in their pants.

He silently watched the end of the cooking show with Stinky. It was a repeat, with the hostess cooing and crowing about the merits of *natto*—helps your eyesight, your digestive system. She was utterly too peppy and *kawaii* relative to the subject matter. Mas was getting ready to leave, but the program abruptly cut to a familiar face: Amika in some earlier coverage of the World Baseball Classic.

Settling back in the couch, Mas wondered why he'd never really noticed Amika before. As a regular watcher of this news program, he must have seen her. It wasn't that she was forgettable. She had a long face with smooth, pale skin and hair past her shoulders. She was definitely attractive in a certain way, but then all these newscasters, especially the female ones, had to be. Perhaps it was her reading of the script. It was refined and warm, nothing like Amika was in person. On the program she was a congenial robot, while her real persona was much more unpredictable.

Mas watched a montage of images, including Amika eating a Dodger dog with Tommy Lasorda and Vin Scully, and Amika showing off a poster signed by pitcher Hideo Nomo. And then there she was, wearing the smeared blue polka-dotted blouse and interviewing Jin-Won Kim after the first game on Tuesday. It wasn't her words that transfixed Mas, but what she was holding to her chest with her left hand. A notebook. It could have been any notebook, a generic notebook, except for the writing on its cover: 帝亜

Emperor of Asia.

Mas abruptly rose, almost toppling some puzzle pieces on a folding table. "I needsu to go," he announced to no one in particular.

He was by the locked door, pressing a button for the nurse to let him out, when Stinky called out, "Hey, Mas." His voice was not as high-pitched as before. It was low and grating like a broken tail pipe scraping the ground. It sounded like the old Stinky.

Mas turned, and Stinky lobbed the baseball right at his head. He didn't have time to catch it, and it landed squarely on his forehead.

Stinky cackled and said, "Good catch."

★ ★ ★

Mas now had a swollen red bump on his head, thanks to Stinky. The nursing-home worker gave him the baseball, castigating him for bringing such a potentially dangerous object into the facility. *Nobody got hurt,* Mas wanted to say. *Nobody except me.* Mas began to wonder if Stinky really had Alzheimer's, or maybe he was thumbing his nose at all of them. A grand final gesture.

One thing was for sure. He needed to talk to Amika. Luckily, Little Tokyo was only a fifteen-minute drive away. Mas passed aging city buildings with low-slung roofs and stunted palm trees that hadn't decided whether to die or try to press on toward the sky.

He first parked at the Miyako Hotel and went in to see

if Amika was there. She still had a room but didn't answer the phone when the front desk called for him. He knew of one other place to check.

The Far East Café, or Entoro, still had its neon sign and old façade, but they were the only things that had stayed the same. A narrow alley in between seismically retrofitted buildings revealed an outdoor bar filled with probably the same youngsters who frequented Suehiro's after midnight.

Sitting at one of the iron-rod tables was a slim figure in a gauzy dress and sneakers. Two empty shot glasses sat in front of her.

"So are you here to interrogate me, too? Have a seat. Have at it." Amika gestured to the seat across from her.

Mas accepted her offer, and when she got a good look at his face, she asked, "What happened to your forehead?"

"Nuttin'. Just bumped in car."

A young waitress with cat-eye makeup and her hair in a bandana came to take his order, but he waved her off. He wasn't planning to stay long.

"I seezu your report today," he said.

"Oh, the wonderful World Baseball Classic."

"Itai, the day he died, holdin' a notebook."

"Really? What a shock." Amika's hand began to tremble a bit.

"And then I seezu you on the terebi, holdin' the same notebook."

"A notebook is a notebook is a notebook."

"Not dis one." Mas took the pencil on the table that was supposed to be for sushi orders. On the margins he wrote the character for *teia*, 帝亜. "Dat notebook had dis."

Amika got up to leave the table.

"*Zainichi*," he said, causing her to stop in her sneakers.

She turned slowly. "What the hell did you say?"

"You'zu *Zainichi*."

Amika returned to the table and lowered herself into her chair.

Mas wasn't sure, but he had a hunch. He remembered her linguistic skills at the press conference. Anyone could know a bunch of languages, but Amika seemed especially interested in things Korean.

"You knowsu Korean."

"A lot of Japanese can speak Korean." Amika went into her purse and pulled out some cigarettes. The same young waitress immediately appeared, scolding, "No smoking, ma'am."

Amika zipped up her purse, got up, and stalked out of the bar and down the alley to the street. Mas, leaving a twenty-dollar bill by the empty shot glasses, quickly followed.

"*Ma'am*? Shit, how old do I look?" she said, lighting up her cigarette.

Now that Mas was so close to Amika's face, he could see the fine lines around her mouth and eyes. Before, he thought she was in her thirties, but he now realized that she was at least forty.

"Don't answer that, by the way." She blew cigarette smoke toward the sidewalk along First Street, and a few young women glared at her and waved away the smoke as they passed. "What the hell is wrong with L.A.?" she murmured to herself.

The cigarette seemed to settle her. "So you think I'm a *Zainichi*, huh? What tipped you off? Do I smell like garlic, like those racists say on the internet? I hate kimchi, by the way."

Mas had never met a woman quite like Amika. Mari was strong, but not always so self-directed. Amika, on the other hand, seemed to know exactly what she wanted all the time. As a result, she left a clear trail of who she was.

"Youzu figure out about Neko and her grandma."

"I'm a journalist. That's what I do for a living. And that's what I have done for almost twenty years."

"But youzu wanted to find out. Your *mokuteki*. I seezu your *mokuteki*."

"My motivation? How about yours, old man? Why are you hanging out with this disaster of a reporter, Kimura? Because even you know that he's terrible, right?"

"I'zu know his grandma."

That piece of information seemed to quiet Amika. She dropped her dead stub of a cigarette on the sidewalk, which was marked with an artist's timeline of the history of Little Tokyo. She crossed her arms, ready to listen.

"Her name izu Akemi Kimura. Weezu in Hiroshima together. During the *pikadon*."

"Shit," Amika muttered and her eyes became shiny. For all the prickly thorns on her outside, she was soft inside.

"We gotsu history together."

"I bet you do." Amika gazed out at First Street, the blur of cars, the lights in restaurants, the pedestrians in motion.

"So yes, I'm a *Zainichi* Korean. It's not a big secret or anything. I just don't advertise it." She leaned against the brick wall and lit another cigarette. "We were forced to get Japanese names. I'm still of that era. So Hadashi. Barefoot. That was my father's joke, I guess. To pick the weirdest Japanese name that he could think of. Because that's how he came to Japan. Without even a good pair of shoes to his name."

"Youzu papa and mama all in Japan?"

Amika nodded. "We're in Nagasaki. So we know something about the *pikadon*, too."

Mas's eyes widened. So was Amika a legacy of the atomic blast, too?

"I know my career is coming to an end. Hell, I'm surprised I've even lasted this long. Because it's all about looking *kawaii* in Japan, right? Like a forever-youthful anime character. Believe it or not, Itai inspired me, at least professionally. He took risks. He challenged me. Of course, he could investigate the thing he did because he was working for *Nippon Series* and not for a mainstream outlet. Television journalism is more superficial, based more on my hair and makeup than what might come out of my mouth."

Amika took a final drag of her cigarette, savoring the nicotine moving through her system before she dropped it on the ground and stepped on it. "I know my days at the news desk are numbered. I figured, what the hell, I'll go after the stories that I've always wanted to cover. A female knuckleball pitcher in Hawaii. And then when I'm doing some research, I find out that her father was born in Manchuria. And not only that, but in an orphanage. My mind begins to whirl. It can't be, right? Could it be? Then I come to find out that Jin-Won Kim's assistant had done research at that very same orphanage. We have two talented knuckleball pitchers, and that's not an easy thing to pull off in the pros. It's not only about physical skill, but the mind. Both Jin-Won and Neko can deal with uncertainty, risk. Is it really a surprise that they share the same DNA?"

"Neko's family not happy wiz you."

"No, that's an understatement." Her hands dipped in her bag for another cigarette. "They're furious. Neko's father still denies it. The adoptive grandparents are threatening to sue the station if we air anything about it. Quite a disaster, I would say."

"Sorry," Mas said.

"No reason to be sorry. I'm doing my job if the people I interview are mad at me. I'm supposed to be uncovering the truth, and more times than not, it's a truth that no one really wants to hear."

If the reporter was talking about truth, then Mas would hold her to it. "Howsu about the notebook?" he said, bringing up the reason he was on the lookout for her in the first place.

Amika looked at Mas as if she was seeing him for the first time. "I've underestimated you," she said. She unzipped her bag again, only this time, instead of a pack of cigarettes, she brought out a notebook. The notebook with 帝亜 written on the cover. Itai's notebook. "I took it because I was curious about what he was working on. Take it." She held it out to Mas. "It's not worth anything. It looks like he was just doodling during practice. Probably wasting time before press conferences."

Mas tapped the *kanji* on the cover. "*Teia*, you knowsu about this?"

"Sounds like something those nationalists would come up with. Maybe Itai had some kind of lead? Maybe it was something he couldn't forget." Amika was distracted by a young couple walking arm and arm across the street by a restaurant called Mr. Pizza. "I broke it off with Sawada today, by the way. I figure you knew about that, too. Mas Arai, the invisible man who knows everything. You do make a good detective."

He had been called a detective once before, and he deeply resented it. He hated the thought of sticking his nose into someone else's business. But he also realized that he'd been doing just that ever since that first baseball game between Japan and Korea.

"And for the record, I didn't do it. I didn't kill Itai. And I certainly wouldn't have done anything to harm Mrs. Kim."

Mas believed Amika about the last thing, but frankly, he wasn't sure of the first. Either way, tonight the girl needed someone to believe in her. Mas could at least fake that much.

Chapter Thirteen

When he got home, Mas studied the letters and numbers in Itai's notebook at the kitchen table. The first line was "T HR HR HR." Second line: "S 340 HR 320." And so on.

The back door opened. Lloyd stepped in and took off his work shoes, leaving them by the door.

"Hey, Dad."

"Hallo."

Mas noticed that Lloyd didn't have the weariness of the past couple of days. He seemed tired, but a good tired. "It was a good day," he said, explaining that they'd finished fertilizing the entire field.

Mas grunted. In that way, he and Lloyd were the same. The completion of a hard day's work, especially if it involved readying the soil, was energizing rather than taxing.

"What's that?" Lloyd looked over Mas's shoulder.

"Sumptin."

"I can see that. Related to baseball? If so, a lot of home runs."

Mari, who so far had been quiet in their room, appeared in the kitchen, pulling a suitcase with rolling wheels. "I'm just about packed," she announced.

"Where'su you going?"

"Jill's wedding. This weekend. Didn't I tell you? I guess everything has been so hectic lately. Jill and Iris—remember her?—are getting married. In Canada. Where it's legal."

Mas had forgotten about the wedding and wondered if Tug and Lil had decided to go.

"I figure Tug would have told you," Mari said, not giving Mas a chance to respond. "Jill is convinced that her parents won't show up. I mean, she puts up this tough-girl front, but you know that she's dying inside. She was always their shining star. Remember how Mom used to compare me to her? 'Look at Jill Yamada. Why don't you be like her? Nice girl. Straight As. Going to be a doctor someday.' Only now she's a struggling mixed-media artist who is also a lesbian. Funny how these things work out."

"Mari, don't be like that," Lloyd said.

"No, my mom was always on my case, Lloyd. At least with Dad, there were no expectations. Sometimes it was easier that way."

Mas frowned. He hated when Mari got into these moods. She wanted to punish Mas and Chizuko for all they did wrong. She was often correct in her assessment, but Mas felt that she should at least keep Chizuko out of it; she had no way of fighting back.

"Ease up, okay?" Lloyd continued to try to calm her down.

"I just feel bad for Jill. She needs her parents to back her up. This is going to be one of the most important days of her life, and her parents aren't going to be there."

Mas felt the full burn of irony. He hadn't been there for Mari and Lloyd's wedding, either. But he wasn't given a choice. He hadn't been invited.

"Tug and Lil gotsu their reasons. They don't need to prove nuttin' to Jill. They behind her every step of the way. Sheezu gotsu know dat."

Mari rolled her eyes.

Mas rose with his notebook. "I mighta wanted to go to my daughter's wedding, too, youzu know. People make own decisions. There's nuttin' to do about it."

★ ★ ★

The next morning, Mas forced himself to sleep in. He'd turned off the ringer on his cell phone, but not the vibrator, so now it was practically dancing on his dresser like a hyperactive giant bug. It was probably Yuki; Genessee usually had a seminar with graduate students at UCLA that day. But just in case it was Genessee, Mas, his bones cracking, lifted himself out of bed. Barefoot, he padded over on the carpet to see who wanted his attention. It was no number that he recognized. Without thinking clearly, he flipped open the phone.

"Hallo." Mas's voice was more muffled than usual.

"Masao-*san*. Is that you?"

"Whozu dis?"

"Akemi. Akemi Kimura."

"Ah, ah…" Mas said, eloquent as usual.

"I haven't been able to get in touch with Yukikazu. He gave me your phone number earlier this week. *Sumimasen*, calling you like this."

"Nah, itsu orai. His phone turned out to be no good."

"Did it stop working?"

The story was too long to delve into.

"Is he there with you?"

"Heezu wiz Neko Kawasaki."

"Oh, no," Akemi said. Mas didn't expect that reaction. Akemi obviously knew who Neko Kawasaki was, so shouldn't she be more excited? "He's been so obsessed with her. I thought that by seeing her in person again he'd be more realistic."

Mas didn't know what to say.

"You know that she's going to break his heart, Mas. What would a woman like that want with Yukikazu?"

Akemi had had her moments of being highfalutin' at times, even when she was young. Chizuko would have quipped, *hana ga takai*. That her nose was up in the air.

"Ah, well, heezu nice boy," Mas said, both shocked and mortified that he was coming to Yuki's defense. "Don't hurt nobody's feelings. *Gambatteru*." As soon as Mas finished talking, he knew that he was describing himself.

"That's all well and good that he's trying hard, but that's not enough. What's going to happen when the honeymoon phase wears off? Yukikazu will be by himself. Destroyed."

"Akemi-*san*, I gotsu go," Mas told her. "I tellsu Yukikazu that you called."

★ ★ ★

Mas didn't bother taking a shower. He quickly dressed. In the bathroom, he patted a palmful of Three Flowers oil on top of his head and pushed his dentures into his mouth. *He will be destroyed*, Mas said to himself. *Destroyed.* He shoved the phone and Itai's notebook into the back pockets of the jeans he'd been wearing this week.

He got into the Impala, backed it out of the driveway in record time, and tore down the street. He didn't know quite what he was going to say, but he had to at least try.

He felt like he was driving for a lifetime. Parking was even worse than usual. He'd only gone to the room once before, but it was on the first floor and in the corner, so it was easy to find.

He didn't even wait at the door or bother to knock. He flung it open, finding Genessee at the front of a line of desks all pushed together in the center of the room. About seven seated students stared blankly at him.

"Mas, what are you doing here?"

He took a deep breath. "I'zu been a big *bakatare*." He was indeed a huge fool. "I'zu just too scared. Scared I'zu be destroyed."

"Oh, Mas." Genessee came right up to him, placing her arms around him. "Just open your heart to me. Even a little bit. Nothing bad is going to happen."

And in front of the Origins of Indigenous Music in the Pacific seminar at UCLA, Mas had his very first experience with a public display of affection.

★   ★   ★

After the encounter with Genessee in her class, Mas felt like he could do anything. Or at least should do anything. Like find Tomo Itai's killer.

When he first encountered Itai, Mas didn't care for him one bit. He was like those *kuso*-heads who parked their car in two spots or cut in line at the betting window at the track. No class and no thought for anyone else. Yes, Itai had been like that, but there'd been more to him. Whether it was the *ianfu* or mixed-race minorities, he'd been committed to the underdog. Itai had believed that he could save the world, a motive that was irritating to Mas, but at least in his writing, the journalist wasn't just out for himself. In his effort to make himself out to be a savior, Itai seemed to have done some good along the way.

Mas parked in the lot for the hospital and went to the reception desk to get a sticker with Mrs. Kim's room number written on it.

He was walking down the hallway toward her room when someone called out, "Arai-*san*." Yuki was seated in the open waiting room with the two knuckleball-pitching cousins.

"This is Mas Arai. She has helped me so much," Yuki introduced Mas to both Neko and Jin-Won in English. Mas at first balked at being identified as "she," but what could he say? He'd lived in America for fifty years himself and still wasn't getting words right. He could ignore a wrong pronoun, especially since he was being paid a compliment.

Mas shook Neko's hand and then Jin-Won's. He had to admit that it was a thrill to touch the hands of professional baseball pitchers. English had to be the language of record, linking the Japanese, Korean, and American together.

"Howsu your grandma?" he asked both Neko and Jin-Won.

Neko's face flushed pink, and at first Mas thought he had said something wrong. Maybe to have identified that intimate relationship so clearly was a mistake.

Neko fanned her hand in front of her face, signaling that she wasn't offended. "No, it's the first time for me to hear that. Grandma. It is so...so like family."

Jin-Won squeezed Neko's shoulder. "Would you like to see?" he asked Mas.

Mas didn't know what to say. It wasn't like he didn't want to see Mrs. Kim, but he barely knew her. He was here for support, to be in the background. Not to be a participant.

"*Ojisan*, go," Yuki said. And then he added in Japanese, "I've told her about you."

Mas took a few steps into the hospital room. Mrs. Kim was lying down, a sheet and blanket up to her chin. She was wearing glasses and her eyes were expectant, ready to see what was around the corner.

"Hallo," Mas said.

"*Konnichiwa*," she replied, and they both laughed in

recollection of their first meeting.

He placed his hands in his jacket pockets. His right hand felt the hard outline of the baseball he'd found in Dodger Stadium. He drew it out.

"You play?" she asked in Japanese.

"When I was a boy. A long, long time ago."

"May I?" She gestured toward the ball, and Mas was only too happy to present it to her. She gripped it in her right hand, blue veins extending from her knuckles, and then palmed it in her left. "I played, too. In school. I was pretty good."

Mochiron, Mas thought. No doubt. Her genes had been passed down to her grandchildren.

She studied him for a moment through her glasses. "You are a *hibakusha*."

Mas nodded.

"It must have been so sorrowful for you."

Mas felt blindsided by Mrs. Kim's comment. "I try not to think about it."

"Me, too," Mrs. Kim said. "All these years, me, too. All these years, I see women outside the Japanese Embassy in Seoul. Protesting what had happened during World War II. Fruitless, I think. Useless. But now I think that I was wrong. I need to tell my story. If I didn't, I wouldn't have ever found my granddaughter, Neko. If I keep talking, who else will I find?"

Mas wanted to warn her that there were people out there, people in the unknown, anonymous internet, who might want to hurt her. But perhaps it was like boxing with shadows. What was the use of always being afraid of a shadow?

"I'm not like you," Mas told her.

Feeling like this meeting had come to an end, Mas bowed his good-bye.

"Sayonara," she said, returning the baseball to him.

As soon as he stepped out of the room, he noticed that someone had been standing by the doorway. Sally Lee, without her camera. She'd most likely been eavesdropping, spying on him the whole time. Mas lowered his head, trying to look as inconspicuous as possible, but Sally called out to him, her voice stripped of its previous hard edges. "I have to apologize," she said. "I was a bit harsh with you the other day. She's been so hurt by Japanese men in the past. I want to make sure it doesn't happen again."

Mas grunted in reply. He didn't like to be stirred into the same pot as pieces of trash. Sally Lee didn't know him, and he didn't know her. But he was getting to know Mrs. Kim. And for her, he accepted the apology.

Mas returned to the waiting room, the baseball in his hand.

"What is that?" Jin-Won asked.

"Oh, found dat in outfield." He tossed it to Jin-Won. Probably would make more sense in the pitcher's possession than in his. Neko looked on, but Yuki was nowhere to be seen.

"Where'su Yuki?"

"The police have him," Neko said.

Mas's back stiffened.

"I'm sorry, I didn't mean it like that. They're here and they had some follow-up questions for him. I'm sure it's just routine."

Mas breathed in and out. With police detectives, nothing was routine.

Neko and Jin-Won took turns holding the ball. They held it as Smitty had shown Mas, with the thumb down and the index and third fingers stretched out like a claw.

Neko kept shaking her head. "*Okashii.*" Strange? What was strange?

She turned to Mas. "The grip. It feels off. Maybe this ball is defective in some way. Hit too many times." Yet the outside skin was perfectly white.

"Mista Mas, you have a knife?" Jin-Won asked.

Did Mas look like some kind of *bakatare* to bring a knife into a hospital? And then he remembered that he did in fact have his pocketknife with him.

Jin-Won took Mas's pocketknife, opened it, and started to cut into the skin of the ball. *This would not do*, Mas thought. Jin-Won's hands were worth millions, while Mas's garnered him a hundred dollars on a good day. "I'zu do it," he said.

He jiggled the short blade for a while, and finally the insides of the ball were released. Mas was surprised to see many skeins of white yarn wrapped around an orange rubber center. Stabbing into the center revealed a cork. He wasn't sure how often professional players dissected their baseballs, but it seemed like Jin-Won had done it before.

"This rubber," Jin-Won fingered the solid core, "seems different. More compact."

"What are you saying?" Neko asked. "That it's been tampered with?" She looked for the manufacturer of the ball on the loose leather skin. "That's a famous company. They wouldn't do illegal things."

"How about the name? The baseball commissioner?" Jin-Won traced the signature of the Japanese professional league's leader.

"I don't know. I don't know," Neko murmured. "Maybe a prototype or something."

Mas then remembered the list of numbers in Itai's notebook. He pulled out the notebook, flipping the cover over to reveal what Itai had written.

"These numba and letters. Maybe how far ball was hit."

"Could be." Neko furrowed her brow. "T, Tanji. S, Sawada." She went down the line, naming all the Japanese players. "So many home runs. Zahed is not mentioned, so maybe he was pitching?"

Mas remembered how Tanji had berated him for his performance at practice. Maybe it wasn't Zahed's fault. Maybe it was the ball's.

"I haven't played with a Japanese ball in long time," said Neko. "Maybe it's just my imagination?"

Their attention to the dissected ball was interrupted by Yuki's return to the waiting room.

He fell into one of their uncomfortable chairs, his skinny legs stretched out on the linoleum. "They believe that

Itai-*san* killed himself. And I think I just confirmed it."

"*Honto*?" Mas could not believe it.

For Jin-Won's benefit, Yuki attempted a few sentences in English. "He met a yakuza who owns a sushi bar in Rosu Angelesu on Monday night. Somewhere called San Fernando." He continued in Japanese. "The police asked me if I had heard of him. I had. He'd been a source for one of Itai's stories five years ago.

"Apparently this yakuza has sold a bunch of drugs, in addition to being involved in some other illegal activities. I told the police that Itai-*san* wasn't into that. Then they tell me that they've been looking into Itai-san's finances. Hardly anything in his bank account. He'd taken out a sizable amount before he left for Los Angeles."

"So?" Mas said.

"The police think that Itai-*san* was preparing to die here."

"Was he?" Neko asked. "I didn't know him very well."

"No, no, no. And that's what I told the detectives."

"Did the yakuza kill him?" Jin-Won interjected, unaware of what had just been communicated in Japanese.

"I do not think so," Yuki replied in English, and then in Japanese. "But Itai-*san* was indeed at a sushi bar in the San Fernando Valley on Monday night. They found video footage."

The police were doing their due diligence, Mas thought. And here he'd thought that Detective Williams and his disagreeable partner were just playing around.

"The yakuza told the police that Itai-*san* was just paying

a social call. But why would he go over there right after arriving in Los Angeles?" Yuki sat forward, cupping his chin with his hands. "And that's not even the worst of it. Some college kid was in there around the same time. Took a selfie of himself and his girlfriend and posted it on Facebook. Itai-*san* was in the background. They blew up the photo and yes, he was receiving some sort of envelope from the yakuza. The police think that's how Itai-*san* got the cyanide."

"Maybe weezu go ova there," Mas chimed in. This information was confusing. Might as well as get it from the horse's mouth.

"That's exactly what I was thinking, *Ojisan*."

★   ★   ★

Mas was in a sense a Valley man, but his valley was the San Gabriel one, the valley held in by purple-tipped mountains. Old money—grand estates and libraries—had first attracted Japanese gardeners, domestics, and laundries to this valley, but now the area was a magnet for new Asian immigrants, not from Japan but from China, Taiwan, and Korea.

The more famous valley in Los Angeles was the San Fernando Valley, a sprawl that didn't seem to have a clear beginning or end. Northwest of San Gabriel, the San Fernando Valley was like a thoroughbred horse that galloped across the dust of Southern California. In places like Pacoima, Roscoe, and Tropico, Japanese farmers had once tended flower fields of ranunculus and anemone and rows of lettuces and carrots. That was all gone now, of course, long cleared to make way for housing developments and shopping malls.

Mas had been to a ramen house in North Hollywood, but in general he tried to limit his time in the Valley. It was strange and unknown to him, filled with impatient, speeding motorists who were quick on their horns. One was currently on his bumper as he traveled west on the 101. And he was in the slow lane.

He and Yuki were on their way to see a yakuza, and Mas didn't know quite what to make of it. He had come across his share of *chimpira*, low-level gangsters in post-atomic Hiroshima. They specialized in the black market as well as drugs, most specifically *hiropon*, heroin. They lassoed young, aimless *hibakusha* who were uncertain about their futures in the rubble of Hiroshima. Once these men and women were caught, it was hard to leave the embrace of money, drugs, and/or pseudo family. The cost of escape was high.

Now they were voluntarily going to enter the den of a gangster. Maybe this was the appropriate way to close their investigation into the death of Tomo Itai. To discover that the demon that had ended the journalist's life was the journalist himself.

Yuki had downloaded directions to the restaurant onto Itai's laptop. Mas had to rely on Yuki to guide him. The off-ramp and main streets were all unfamiliar to him. If, somehow, they became separated from the power of the laptop, Mas would be trapped and hopelessly lost in this valley, which was as mysterious to him as the moon.

From the outside, the sushi bar more closely resembled a bar than a restaurant. Inside, it was the more of the same.

The walls were covered in dark wood; the carpet was a blood red. The expansive sushi bar must have originally been built to accommodate more mixed drinks than tuna rolls, and the bar was adorned with plenty of both. It was three-thirty, in between lunch and dinner, a time when the typical Japanese restaurant was closed. But this place was obviously not typical.

Yuki pointed to the *itamae-san* at the end of the bar. "That's him," he whispered in Mas's ear. Mas wanted to tell the boy not to point, but it was too late now.

A *hakujin* couple—a woman in a low-cut top and leather pants and a man dressed all in black—sat in front of the yakuza chef. Mas was surprised to see that he was tattoo-less and slight. He probably weighed the same as Mas, give or take a few pounds. But he was at least half a foot taller, with wispy, shaggy hair and a faint afternoon shadow above his lip and on his chin.

Like all traditional sushi chefs, he wore all white, including a white apron that was tied high on his waist, but instead of the typical white skull hat, he wore a bandana that had an image of the rising sun.

After the diners finally left, Yuki and Mas took their places. The yakuza chef seemed surprised that they didn't wait to sit until the dirty plates were removed from the bar.

"*Irrashaimase*," the chef said to welcome them, as a waitress hurriedly cleared the dirty dishes. "What will you have?"

"I am a friend of Tomo Itai," Yuki said, skipping the small talk.

The chef scrunched up his long nose as if he smelled something rotten. "Get out," he said. "The cops have already wasted enough of my time. You can speak to my lawyer if you want."

"I worked as a reporter with Itai-*san*. On the same stories. I know you were a source for his series about yakuza in America five years ago. I'm sure your colleagues back in Japan wouldn't be too happy to hear about your cooperation."

The chef picked up one of his knives. It looked freshly sharpened and glinted from the lights above the bar. "Follow me." He headed toward the kitchen in back but then stopped, gesturing to Mas. "Not him."

"I go where he goes," Mas said in Japanese.

The chef's mouth curved into an ugly smile. "I was just trying to spare you, *Ojisan*. You want to play? C'mon."

Mas swallowed and followed the chef into the kitchen, with Yuki pulling up the rear. The top of Mas's head barely touched the indigo blue *noren,* the rectangular fabric hanging from the kitchen's entryway. Inside were mostly Latinos, like in any restaurant in Southern California, busy cutting cabbage and washing dishes.

The chef led them into a back room. This was not good, Mas knew. Sure, there were workers just a few feet away, but they were the yakuza's employees, and they were probably used to ignoring illegal activities going on behind closed doors. Sure enough, as soon as Mas stepped inside, the chef pushed him against the bare wall, his sashimi knife grazing the stubble on Mas's chin.

"I'll slice this old man's throat," the chef said, as if he

were boasting. Although the light was faint in the room, Mas noticed a scar by the chef's nose. He must have been cut some time ago. Violence was nothing new to this man. "I want you out of my place, and you will never bother me again. You say anything to the police or my friends in Japan, and I'll hunt this old man down." He nodded toward the back door, an iron security gate, clearly expecting Yuki to immediately take the opportunity to leave.

Yuki didn't budge. Mas didn't know whether to be impressed or incensed. It was literally his neck on the line here.

"The police have already spoken to me, too," Yuki said. "Detective Williams, right? I told him that Itai-*san* wouldn't have bought any drugs from you. Especially something like cyanide."

Mas felt the chef's grip loosen a little. He was listening.

"I asked them for proof. Solid proof. They had a photo taken by a customer who'd posted it on Facebook. Of you giving Itai something in an envelope. What was in that envelope?"

The chef let Mas go and set the knife on a desk by the door. He took a deep breath and started talking. "It was a memory card. From a camera. With photos of Soji Zahed. I had a party here in his honor and a stupid paparazzi took a photo of him, let's say, enjoying himself. He was going to sell those photos to the tabloids, which, of course, would have ruined his chances with the majors. Itai paid me to take care of it and get that memory card. So I did."

Mas wondered what "taking care of it" meant.

"My regular bouncer would never have let that *papar-*

rachi in my place."

"Why didn't you just tell the police that? That Itai-*san* was just after the photos?"

"And what? Spill the beans on Zahed? I told Itai that I'd keep quiet."

Mas knew that the yakuza had their own code of ethics. He'd heard that gangster culture had been changing in Japan, but maybe here in the US, like all things Japanese, the yakuza clung to their old-school traditions, afraid that if they lost hold of them, their identity would also slip away.

The chef grabbed his sashimi knife. "I'm a man of my word. Itai knew it. And I'm sorry that he's dead. Now get the hell out of here."

★ ★ ★

When they returned to the Impala, Yuki asked to use Mas's phone. He looked up a phone number on Itai's laptop and dialed it. "Zahed," he said. "It's Kimura. I need to talk to you. Immediately. Where are you?" Mas heard a slight mumble coming from his phone, held to Yuki's ear. "Um, um," Yuki grunted a few times. And then, "Wait for me. I'll meet you at the parking lot."

"He's at Dodger Stadium," he told Mas.

"What we gonna do when we see him?"

"Find out if he did it. If he killed Itai-*san*."

"But if Itai was helping him—"

"Maybe Zahed didn't know what had happened with the photos."

He did seem desperate to get ahold of Itai's computer, Mas remembered.

Zahed was waiting by a five-foot red number 42, a tribute to Jackie Robinson. He hurried over to the Impala as soon Mas pulled into a space. Yuki rolled down his window, because it was obvious that Zahed wanted to tell him something. "Not here," Zahed said. "Somewhere else in the parking lot."

"Get in," Yuki told him.

Mas drove the Impala through the huge lot, far, far away from the other cars. He stopped by the edge of the Japanese garden. Just being next to it made him feel more settled.

"Can we talk? Just you and me," Zahed said to Yuki.

Mas didn't mind leaving the car. Zahed got into the driver's seat, and Mas was careful to make sure that he took the keys. Who knows how the teenage *senshu* would respond to Yuki's accusations?

The conversation was obviously not going well. The voices in the Impala rose, and the whole car began to shake.

Out the driver's-side door came Zahed. He sprinted away with Itai's laptop underneath his arm.

"Give that back!" Yuki shouted in Japanese, chasing after him. "That's not going to save you!"

There was really no place to run in the wide-open parking lot, so Zahed headed for the fenced garden. He pulled at the gate, and as Mas had discovered earlier, it swung open easily.

"*Chikusho*," Yuki cursed. He followed the pitcher through the gate and up a dirt path toward the garden. It was full-on dusk, with the sun below the horizon.

Kiyotsuke, Mas said under his breath. The untended garden was a minefield of potholes. Worse in the dark, without even the distant glow of the stadium lights. Chavez Ravine at night when there wasn't a baseball game going on was indeed a dark ravine, one that threatened to unleash ghosts of the buried past.

"Shit!" Yuki's voice rang out.

Mas, his hands shaking, dialed his cell phone. "Lloyd. Come to Japanese garden. *Hayaku*." He wasn't sure if he made any sense or not. Either way, he couldn't just stand there and wait by the car.

He cursed himself for not having a flashlight in the Impala. One was in his toolbox that he kept at the McAdams's Hollywood Hills estate. What good did that do him now?

Holding onto the bars of the iron fence for balance, Mas gingerly climbed up the dirt path. He wanted to call out to Yuki, but he knew it would only signal his location to Zahed. When he'd almost reached level ground, he nearly tripped on something. Something grabbed his leg, but before he could cry out, he heard, "*Ojisan*, it's me."

Mas bent down, his knees popping. Yuki whispered, "I think I might have sprained my foot."

They heard something up above, and Mas thought he spied movement by the concrete *toro*.

He remembered the granite memorial for Korean immigrants that was nearby and helped Yuki crawl over to it for cover.

"Your cell phone, *Ojisan*?"

Mas pulled it out for Yuki, who opened it and groaned. "Damn, no service here. It's like a black hole."

"Who's that? Kimura?" Zahed called out.

"Just give it up, Soji-*kun*," Yuki yelled. "If you just co-operate, they'll go easy on you."

"Why should my career be ruined over this?"

Mas saw the outline of Zahed's long body making its way toward them.

"Shit," Yuki murmured.

Mas felt around the ground for anything—a stone he could throw, loose dirt that could temporarily blind Zahed's eyes. He found a branch that had fallen from one of the dried-up trees on the hill.

"My whole life has been devoted to baseball. My parents sacrificed everything for me. I'm not going to let this ruin that." Yuki was now a few feet away. Zahed held the computer over his head, ready to plunge it down the hill. Mas grabbed hold of the branch and dragged it forward as hard as he could. It hit the back of Zahed's foot, causing him to fall backward onto his behind.

A line of light pierced through the darkness of the garden, resting on Zahed's fallen body. Zahed looked more stunned than hurt, and he covered his eyes with the crook of his arm.

"What the hell is going on here?" Lloyd asked, holding onto a high-powered flashlight.

"Watch him, Arai-*san*," Yuki said.

Mas stood up and dug the branch into Zahed's stomach.

"Zahed kill Itai-*san*," Yuki announced in English.

That statement revived Zahed. He easily knocked the branch from Mas's grasp and scrambled up from the dead pine needles. "*What?* No. I would have never hurt Itai-*san*. He was like a father to me."

"Then why did you run up here with Itai-*san*'s computer?" Yuki asked, using the base of the memorial to get to his feet.

"I thought those photos of me were on his laptop. He told me that if I didn't behave myself in the future, he'd release them. I wanted to make sure they didn't end up in the wrong hands."

Lloyd had stopped listening to the conversation. He was aiming his flashlight toward the ten-foot *toro*, the cemetery of dead trees, and the slopes covered with brown pine needles.

"So what happens now?" Zahed asked.

Indeed, what happens, wondered Mas.

"Well, first of all, you stay put in Los Angeles," said Yuki.

"I live in Rancho Cucamonga, so I'm not going anywhere."

"Where's Rancho Cucamonga?" Yuki whispered in Mas's ear.

"Itsu not too far."

"You'll have to tell the police exactly what Itai-*san* did for you."

"No! It'll get out to the team managers."

"Do you want the police to say that Itai-*san* killed himself? Do you think that will honor his memory? They'll stop looking for his murderer if you don't tell the truth."

"I didn't think about that," Zahed said.

"No, you were just thinking about yourself," Yuki shot back. "I was like you at one time. Totally self-centered. But working with Itai-*san* taught me that I cannot be the center of the story. The story always has to be about other people."

Mas couldn't believe what he was hearing. Yuki, who was barely a decade older than Zahed, had grown up. And it looked like that had happened under Itai's tutelage.

Yuki picked up the laptop, and the four of them made their way out of the Japanese garden and back to the parking lot. Zahed got in a golf cart with Lloyd, while Mas found the business card of that LAPD detective, Cortez Williams.

"We won't tell anyone about those photos," Yuki said to Mas in the Impala. "We can ask the police not to mention it in their report. Itai-*san* would have wanted it that way. For his sake, we need to keep quiet. This will be my gift to honor my *senpai*."

Chapter Fourteen

I can't help but think that I've failed Itai-*san*." Yuki said from his spot in a sleeping bag on Mas's bedroom floor.

Mas wished the boy would shut up and sleep, but he was clearly too wired from their encounter in the Japanese garden. Luckily, Detective Williams answered his cell phone and agreed to meet Zahed at the police station. Yuki wanted to stay, but Mas convinced him to crash at his house in Altadena. His ankle needed attention; Lloyd helped by cooling it with Blue Ice and settling him in a spot where he could elevate his leg. Takeo served as Yuki's personal butler, running to retrieve a towel from the linen closet to wrap the ice to mitigate the coldness.

Lloyd also had been energized, not by the conflict but by the setting. As he'd never gone over to the pitiful Japanese garden before, every corner of it fascinated him. After tending to Yuki's foot, he began sketching out the garden on a piece of graph paper, calculating where to build additional slopes in the dirt that had been flattened by the elements. Maybe he'd even build a koi pond.

Mas sighed. "Youzu figure out Zahed's secret," he said to Yuki. "You knowsu about Missus Kim being Neko's grandma. No mo' mystery." He didn't mention anything about Amika being a *Zainichi* Korean. He figured that was Amika's personal business; she could reveal it whenever she wanted to.

"But we still don't know who killed Itai-*san*. And the police are probably going to label it a suicide. That's something a traditional Japanese would do. Not Itai-*san*. He didn't care that he didn't have a penny to his name. He didn't care about such things."

"Just *nenasai*," Mas admonished him to sleep. "Nuttin' we can do now."

Mas felt like he'd slept only for a few hours when Yuki started talking again. "*Ojisan*, can we use your computer printer? I saw one in the living room."

Mas cracked open his eyes and saw sunlight coming through the slats of the blinds, so it was later than he thought. "Yah, go ahead." He returned to his pillow.

Yuki wasn't moving. "Not sure how to set it up."

Mas sat up, took a deep breath, and pushed himself erect. His bare feet carried him to Mari and Lloyd's bedroom. He knocked, saying, "Mari, we needsu your help."

She opened the door immediately. "What? Oh, good morning," she greeted both Mas and Yuki, carrying laundry in her arms. Mas checked the clock in her room. Past the time Takeo was taken to school. "How's your foot? Lloyd told me you injured it last night."

"Okay," Yuki said. "Not too bad."

"He needsu to print sumptin," Mas interrupted.

She set down the clothes she'd been folding. "Sure."

Mas returned to his bed, but he couldn't get back to sleep. He heard the two of them speaking in broken English and broken Japanese, attempting to forge some kind of communication. Then he heard the printer humming and spinning its gears. Mas finally got out of bed again to see what was going on.

Mari was standing over the printer, checking how the paper was feeding.

Mas walked into the living room in his worn-out slippers, the same ones he wore when Chizuko was alive. Yuki looked up. "I've made my own notes on Itai's computer," he explained to Mas. "Just seeing if I've missed something here."

Yuki's notes were in Japanese. It seemed like he had enough for a book, judging from the number of pages being spit out by the printer. A few pages fell to the floor, and Mari picked them up. One page had a photo of the former Swedish ocean liner, the *Gripsholm*.

"Why do you have a photo of the *Gripsholm*?" she asked.

"You know?" Yuki asked incredulously.

Mas was also surprised.

She turned to her father. "Remember when I was working on that proposal to do a documentary on Japanese Peruvians, like Juanita's parents? They were practically kidnapped during World War II and brought over for a possible prisoner of war exchange. They never left Texas during the war, but a lot of other Japanese Peruvians went on the *Gripsholm*. And Nisei, too. Even children. I guess it may have been the worst for them, having no choice in the matter. It was like they were repatriating to Japan, only their home was really America."

"Itai-*san* do research. Interested in many things."

"Yeah, not many people know about the *Gripsholm* story. I wonder if Itai was able to talk to some of the people who stayed in Japan. I think most of them came back to America."

Mas then remembered what Wishbone had told him. "Went all the way ova to India or sumptin."

Now it was Mari's turn to be impressed. "That's right. That's where they did the transfer of prisoners. Those from America had to get on the *Teia,* and those from Japan went on the *Gripsholm*."

"What you say?" Yuki asked.

"What?"

"Youzu say ' *Teia*'?"

"Yeah, the *Teia*. There were two ships involved—the entire voyage took eight weeks or something—and the *Teia* was pretty rough, as I understand it. May I?" she gestured to the laptop, and Yuki nodded.

Mari pulled the charging laptop toward her as she settled in a chair next to Yuki. "Does this have an English mode?" she asked. Yuki nodded, and after making the adjustments, Mari tapped the keyboard and swiped the trackpad. "Yes, here it is." On the screen was an image of a military ship. On the bow she could see its name painted in both English and

Japanese *kanji*, "*Teia Maru*" and 帝亜丸. Mari read some of the caption. "This ship was formerly the *Aramis*. A French ship. It was taken over in 1942 by the Japanese and renamed *Teia*."

Mas found Itai's notebook underneath the papers and pointed to the *kanji* on its cover and also on the back of the laptop. "*Teia*."

Mari pursed her lips. "Wow, he was obsessed with it. The ship wasn't just a passing interest. He must have been connected to it personally somehow."

Mas agreed. But Itai was too young to have been on it himself.

Mari was getting drawn into the mystery. "Wait, let me find my research." She retrieved her laptop from her bedroom and they waited as it booted up.

"I have the ship's manifest here somewhere. So what's his family name again?"

"Itai," Mas said and then corrected himself. "Look for Hirose."

"Hirose. Yup. There're four. Bunjiro, Tsuyo, Kanzo, and Hideaki." She also had information about their ages. Bunjiro and Tsuyo were father and mother, respectively. Kanzo was sixteen, Hideaki was twelve.

"Not Sunny." Mas frowned.

"Well, Sunny is obviously a nickname."

Mas thought of the two possible Japanese characters for Hideaki. It could be "excellent" or could be "light." He and Yuki were on the same wavelength. "Hideaki," they said in unison.

"Why Sunny say nothing?" Yuki said in English.

Yes, Mas thought. He'd mentioned the camp in Arizona, but nothing about being in Japan, even when Mas mentioned that he himself was there during the war.

"Maybe he was hiding it for some reason," Mari said.

"Of all the documents on Itai-*san*'s computer and thumb drive, it was the *Gripsholm* folder that was erased." Yuki bit his fingernail in thought.

And who'd had access to the computer and thumb drive? Sunny.

"Did you check Itai's email inbox and outbox?" Mari asked.

Yuki was able to follow that much of Mari's English. "Yes. That empty, too."

He began twirling his finger on the computer's track pad and clicked a couple of times. "*Chotto matte.* An email came in a couple of days ago."

Mari got up and read the message out loud over Yuki's shoulder: "Dear Mr. Itai, I'm sorry we could not meet last Tuesday. I've since returned to Hawaii. I've tried to contact you via phone, but I've received no response.

"I have to admit that I was very disappointed in your change of heart concerning the manuscript. Our editorial board was very excited about your cousin's memoir, as stories about Japanese Americans on the prisoner exchange ship the *Gripsholm* are rare."

"There's a mention and attachment of a manuscript in a previous correspondence," Yuki said. He lowered his head toward the bottom of the screen and slowly read in English:

"*The* Teia *Chronicles: The Memoir of an American on a Prisoner Exchange Ship during World War II*, by Kanzo Hirose."

Mari looked back at her computer screen, where the list of the *Gripsholm* manifest was displayed. "That must be him. Hideaki's older brother."

"*Chotto*," Yuki said, after running his fingertips on the trackpad. "Itai-*san* make message."

Mas got out his glasses and joined the two in front of the screen to read Itai's original message:

Dear Mr. Niiya,

I've had a change of heart. I would like to withdraw my manuscript about my late cousin's experience on the Gripsholm.

I am cancelling my meeting with you tonight.

Sincerely,

Tomo Itai

"He sent this on his phone," Yuki pointed to some minuscule numbers and letters. "Itai-*san* sent this on the day he was killed. Very early on Tuesday morning."

"He must have been very close with his cousin," Mari commented.

"Whyzu you say dat?"

"Well, I mean, he's obviously representing his late cousin's interests." She turned to Yuki. " 'Late' means dead. Usually a closer surviving relative, like a child, would receive the rights to such a document."

"Howzu about brotha?" Mas said.

"If this Sunny is indeed Kanzo's brother, then, yeah, I wonder why Itai was representing the memoir and not Sunny."

★ ★ ★

Mari wanted them to call the police, but Mas declined. They'd gone through so much for Yuki's investigation. They deserved to see Sunny's reaction face to face.

They didn't bother to call first. It would be better to catch the old man off guard. And besides, what would a seventysomething retired bachelor be doing on a late weekday morning?

Yuki and Mas assumed correctly, because Sunny's Toyota Corolla was parked in the driveway. The garage was presumably stuffed with junk, based on Sunny's interior decoration.

He came to the door with a half-eaten tuna sandwich in one hand. "Hello," he said congenially. After studying Yuki's and Mas's faces, his own became more grim.

"Come in, come in," he said, leaving the door ajar and walking through his maze of possessions.

He threw his corner of bread crust into the kitchen sink and rejoined his guests in his living room. "*Ocha*?" he asked, offering green tea again, although he seemed to know there'd be no takers.

Mas was trapped next to the table and bench that he first thought was for woodworking. Some kind of sanding drum was attached to the table, and then he remembered seeing the exact same contraption in the garage of a customer who had a side business making jewelry. His customer's work involved all sorts of chemicals—some of them semi-lethal—that he'd been careful to store. In fact, he often told Mas to take care when he walked through the garage into the backyard.

"You'zu make jewelry wiz dis thing," Mas said abruptly. Yuki glared as if to ask, *What are you doing?*

Sunny steadied himself with a stack of boxes.

"Lotsu of chemical involved in dis machine."

Yuki quickly caught on. "Cyanide, *Ojisan?*"

"You don't want your brotha's book published, so you killsu your cousin," Mas declared.

Sunny looked out the top of the living room window, a forlorn look on his face. Now his round face resembled more the moon than the sun.

"That wasn't his book to make decisions about. My brother Kan is dead, and so are our parents. I'm the only living one in my brother's memoir. It wasn't right for Tomo to give it to the publisher without my permission."

So Sunny was indeed Hideaki.

"Did you read the book? Since you know about it, you must have," said Sunny. "I couldn't get past the first thirty pages."

Mas had no idea what was in that manuscript. But he figured that whatever it was, it brought up memories that Sunny wanted to forget.

"I hated being on those ships." Sunny's back and arms

now leaned against the boxes of soy sauce. "The *Gripsholm*, but more the *Teia*. It was like a floating prison with no room to sleep. No water for showers, so we had to sit out on the deck when it rained to wash our bodies. And it was bitterly cold, with no decent food. Our rice had worms in it. When I was a little boy, I dreamed of traveling to wild and exotic places, but not like that."

Gohan with worms? Mas remembered those times of want.

"I came back to the US as soon as I could. But I told no one that I was on the *Gripsholm*. Nobody understood that we hadn't renounced our citizenship. We weren't being repatriated to Japan, and we weren't POWs. We were kidnapped. I was drafted during the Korean War and was happy to fight for America. I put my past, the *Gripsholm* and the *Teia*, behind me." He grasped his right fist in his left hand, the rings on his fingers shining in the morning sun.

"Now Tomo was going to spill the beans about my private life while I'm trying to enjoy my retirement? My war buddies won't read my brother's memoir, but they'd hear about it. I'll be forever connected to the *Gripsholm*." It was obvious that Sunny was scared out of his mind about his secret past being revealed. Had he been looking over his shoulder his whole life?

"Do you know how many men in my unit during the Korean War were either killed or wounded in action? Everyone talks about World War II or even the Vietnam War, but we lost a lot of men in the Korean War, too. I'm a patriot. Will people remember that?"

Sunny was now sitting on the floor, his possessions crowded around him, possessing him. He looked like he had melted, collapsed from his memories. Mas could relate, but his pain was no justification for murder.

"We go to police, Hirose-*san*," Yuki said, helping the old man to his feet.

Sunny realized that it was time. "Yes, yes," he said. "But I need a ride."

Chapter Fifteen

Y ou know that Tomo had the nerve to tell me that I was an awful brother to Kan. That I never visited him when he was ill. But I swore when I left Japan that I'd never go back." Now that he was out of his cluttered home and freed from the weight of his physical possessions, Sunny Hirose had become an *oshaberi*. Words flowed in the Impala. There'd been a lot on Sunny's mind all these years, and admitting that he'd killed his cousin seemed to have given him permission to release all his demons.

"My father, who owned a small dry goods store in Bakersfield, was hopping mad at America," he said from the passenger seat. "Why would they send him and our family as pawns in a prisoner exchange with Japan? He was from Japan but he had no special allegiance to the country. We were on those two godforsaken boats for almost two months. Once we arrived in Japan, we saw the country's true condition. Bombed out, poorer than poor."

Mas traveled down the 10, a river of cars heading for different destinations. Most were likely mundane. Work in a skyscraper or a hospital. College. Lunch with a friend. At least one gardening truck heading for a customer. And here Mas was, transporting a murderer to the police.

"My parents were beaten down. They weren't even quite sure why we were selected to go on the *Gripsholm*. It's not like they wanted to repatriate or anything. My father was one of the early ones to get picked by the US government right after the bombing of Pearl Harbor. Got sent to Bismarck, North Dakota, for a few months before joining us in Gila River. Maybe somehow he got on a list then. A vulnerable man who could be used as a chess piece. The government didn't have enough desirable prisoners to trade with Japan. So they crammed these boats with Japanese Peruvians and assorted people like us."

Mas glanced at his side mirror as he merged onto the Pasadena Freeway at the Convention Center. There, as a reminder of the beginning of their adventure, he saw the silos of the Bonaventure Hotel.

"My brother eventually met a Japanese girl and decided that he wanted to make a life in Japan. But not me." Sunny pursed his lips, seeming to realize that the LAPD headquarters, Parker Center, was only blocks away.

Parking was limited in downtown L.A., so Mas dropped Sunny and Yuki in front of Parker Center. Mas had heard that Parker Center, with its rectangular shape like a monster toaster, would soon be on its way out. Its brand-spanking-new replacement on First Street, a glass cathedral, gave the illusion of transparency—an illusion, because the glass revealed only interior walls. Mas had no real affinity for Parker

Center, but its light-blue motif and scrawny palm trees represented his Los Angeles. It was a Los Angeles full of hope and possibilities, with simple lines and enough empty space to give newcomers opportunity to add colors of their own. Now Los Angeles was jam-packed with people, and developers were trying to build more on top of more until you couldn't see the sky full-frame.

Instead of going into a pay parking lot, Mas circled south through Little Tokyo. He passed the police parking lot on John Aiso Street, named after a judge who, after an illustrious career, had been mugged at a gas station in Hollywood and thrown down, eventually dying from head injuries. He drove along First Street, remembering Ginza Ya, the dry goods store that put Sunny's hoarding tendencies to shame. There was barely room to walk through that shop, but it had everything Mas and Chizuko needed to build a life in the 1970s. A few doors down there'd been a grocery, which displayed its produce—piles of sweet potatoes, Japanese pears, persimmons, and tangerines—in stands open to the sidewalk, New York–style. On the other side of First had been a tiny bookstore in an insurance building. It sold manga, packaged with projects to make robots and tigers out of paper, alongside slim paperbacks in Japanese. The manga, along with fresh *imagawayaki*, thick hockey pucks of batter enclosing dollops of red bean, had been Mari's favorites as a child.

Mas's phone began to chirp. Yuki was ready to be picked up. Time for Mas's nostalgic reverie to end. His Little Tokyo, aside from the *imagawayaki*, was pretty much gone.

The future awaited.

★   ★   ★

Yuki, joking that he was starting to feel at home at the LAPD, said that Sunny kept running at the mouth while they waited for Detective Cortez Williams in the lobby. He was like a broken faucet, he told Mas in the Impala.

"Maybe in jail heezu can write his own book," Mas quipped, and they both got quiet. Sunny's fate was no laughing matter.

"I didn't have the heart to tell him that Itai-*san* had pulled the book, anyway," said Yuki. "If Itai-*san* had just told Sunny that he was going to abide by his wishes, his life would have been spared."

Mas nodded. Sunny had thought that by killing Itai, he'd be able to keep his past silent. As it turned out, all it did was end his Friday-night poker games with his Korean War buddies. Mas knew of other Japanese men in prison, but they were younger. Sunny would probably die behind bars.

Yuki asked to be driven to Mrs. Kim's nursing home in Koreatown, and Mas complied. He didn't relish battling the congestion on Sixth Street and Western Avenue, but knowing that their time together was coming to an end made the drive bearable.

"*Ojisan*, about your fee," Yuki finally said.

"No *shinpai*." Mas surprised himself by saying that. "Itsu on the house."

"I can't let you do that. I don't have all the cash right

now, but after I file a few stories, I can wire you money from Japan."

Mas respected that Yuki wanted to be *chanto*. *Chanto*, to do things just right, was high on Mas's list of priorities. Mas knew that he missed the perfection mark by a football field, but when it came to paying his bets and helpers like Eduardo, he tried to bat a thousand.

"You knowsu what, give it to Mrs. Kim."

"She's not going to take your money, *Ojisan*. Besides, she has a good pension, not to mention Jin-Won and Neko for support. She's well taken of, financially speaking."

"Well, howsu about dat Sally Lee? Sheezu helpin' out other *ianfu*, *desho*?"

Yuki choked as if he had a piece of chicken bone caught in his throat. "You want to give money to her advocacy work?"

Mas shrugged. Why not?

"You are full of surprises, *Ojisan*," Yuki said. "Every time I think I know what you're going to do, you go in the opposite direction."

"I'm like a koi," Mas said in Japanese, laughing. "Keep trying to swim upstream."

★ ★ ★

Yuki, attempting to read Mas's old Thomas Guide map, instructed Mas to make a right turn after making a right onto Western from Wilshire. Mas felt like he'd won a victory by presenting the book of neighborhoods to Yuki in lieu of the talking GPS. His map book went back to the 1970s, before certain freeways, such as the 105, even existed. And certain pages, like the ones for Silver Lake, were missing from overuse. Mas never truly understood those tangled streets around the reservoir. But the pages for Koreatown were still intact. While the storefronts had changed in this area, the streets themselves had not.

The rehabilitation facility turned out to be a modest bungalow with a tiny parking lot. There were no open spaces for the Impala, and street parking didn't look much better.

"Getsu out. I findsu parking and come later," Mas told Yuki, who was first hesitant to leave Mas on his own.

Mas finally found a spot beside a crumbling curb a good four blocks away. When he approached the nursing home, he saw Yuki and Neko standing outside on the walkway.

"We're moving my grandmother here, to Los Angeles," Neko announced. "To Little Tokyo, in fact. There's a senior housing center next to Asian grocery stores, and it has a hot meal program."

"*Honto*?" Mas was surprised. He thought he would never see Mrs. Kim again. To think that he might run into her at the fish counter of a local grocery store.

"The Dodgers might put in an offer for Jin-Won."

"Oh, yah?" Another surprise.

"But it's too early to report that. Anywhere," Neko admonished Yuki.

He crossed his arms. "I'm thinking of taking a break from journalism."

"But what will you do?"

"Maybe write a book?"

Mas couldn't believe his ears. Now every sonofagun was writing one.

Neko didn't acknowledge Yuki's newfound aspiration to be a book author. "Sally Lee can watch out for my grandmother. My grandmother told me that I'm supposed to call her '*halmoni.*' It's grandma in Korean," she added, smiling as if she was holding something extra sweet in her mouth.

To watch these twentysomething sweethearts, driven by entirely different passions, amused Mas. He didn't know if Yuki and Neko would be together in the next six months—he doubted it—but the inevitable push and pull of their relationship would help chip away at who they really were.

★ ★ ★

Mas left Yuki with Neko and navigated the curves of the Pasadena Freeway until it ended. Then up, up, up until he was almost in the foothills of the San Gabriel Mountains.

Tug's ranch-style house was close to the giant, shedding cedars lining the side streets of Altadena. The trees made for a grand entrance, a reminder that the humans on the ground were truly dwarfed by a nature that could infiltrate even the concrete streets. One day, Mas had discovered a brown bear and her cub splashing in a customer's swimming pool. Another time, during a late-night rainstorm during the holidays, two confused coyotes crossed Mas's path while he was driving. No matter how quickly open lots converted to multi-unit dwellings, nature would not be swept away.

Mas was halfway hoping that no one would be home, but the Yamadas' old Buick, still in pristine shape, sat in the driveway.

Mas rang the doorbell and waited a while, finally hearing the sound of the locks being turned. Lil, her face tense, attempted a smile. "Oh, Tug's not here, Mas."

"Just checkin' on the washing machine."

Her voice softened. "It's good. Perfect. Working great."

"So, Tug went ova to Canada, huh?"

Lil gave in. "Come in, Mas. I just made some banana bread."

Mas followed her into an airy, open kitchen with large windows facing a well-manicured backyard.

"Mari went, I take it," Lil said.

"Lloyd take her to airport dis morning." Mas took a seat at their kitchen table, a fancy number that was part of their kitchen remodel.

"You probably think I'm an awful mother," said Lil, cutting a fat slice of fresh banana bread and placing it on a plate with a fork and knife.

Mas shook his head. Chizuko and Lil had become friends through motherhood. Lil was Jill's perennial cheerleader. While Chizuko's approach was to refrain from complimenting Mari, either publicly or privately, Lil lavished compliments on her only daughter.

"I had just begun to accept that Iris would be in Jill's life. But get married? Mas, I can't be a hypocrite. I can't stand there as mother of the bride and pretend that it's okay with me. I know, I'm terrible. Even Jill's brother says I'm behind the times. That I need to join the twenty-first century." Her voice broke. *Is she going to cry?* he worried.

"It's like my world is slowing down, coming to an end, while the outside is spinning by so fast. I can't even catch my breath."

Mas took a few bites of the banana bread. "*Gomen ne,*" he finally said. "I gotsu go."

Lil wrapped the leftover bread in a napkin and handed it to Mas at the door. "I don't know what's going to happen, afterwards. I can't lose my daughter. She's really my everything." Tears finally ran down her papery face, and Mas didn't know what to say. He had no answers.

"I'zu going to get married again," Mas abruptly announced.

"Oh, Mas, I'm so happy for you. I never told you this, but Chizuko wanted you to find someone." Lil pulled out some tissues from a box on a table near the door and wiped her face. "Well, actually, what she told me was something like, 'No one will want to have that old man, but if someone wants to pick him up, that's okay with me.'"

Mas laughed. He knew that Lil was telling the truth, because that sounded exactly like Chizuko.

"You and Jill figure it out somehowsu," Mas finally said, and he walked down the porch steps. It might take a lifetime, but he had faith that they would.

★ ★ ★

It was Chizuko's birthday, so Mas prepared to do what he always did around this time. Clean her gravesite plot. The last time he went there was right before Valentine's Day. He didn't actually time it for that—in fact, he would have avoided it if he'd realized it earlier. Too many red roses and stuffed teddy bears with hearts, symbols of love that could not be reciprocated by the dead.

Mas had never in his life given his wife red roses, at least on purpose. One time a customer had gotten into a fight with his girlfriend and shoved a bouquet in Mas's dirty hands after he'd mowed the lawn. Chizuko's eyes grew wide when he brought it in through the back door, but they returned to their normal size when he explained what had happened.

Mas didn't even know what day was their official wedding anniversary. There was the day he received her photo in the mail when he was a bachelor gardener in Altadena. And the day he wrote back to his parents saying that he was interested. And the day he actually traveled to Hiroshima to lay eyes on her for the first time as an adult. He'd actually seen her once, before he left Hiroshima. She was the younger sister of a former classmate, and she was only about thirteen at the time. Even at that age, she was very *majime*, serious, but with the loss of her two brothers, she had to be. He'd heard that Chizuko's family had lost everything in the Bomb and were living with distant relatives to make ends meet.

The wedding ceremony and reception were a blur. He'd felt like he was playing dress-up, in his rented tuxedo. Chizuko wore a silky kimono adorned with a giant crane. The *furisode,* long sleeves, almost reached the floor and made Mas feel that he would be knocked over by a wave of passion. The kimono was knotted with a colorful rope in the front, as if Chizuko's insides were being held together, suppressed. Her face pancaked white, she wore the traditional wedding cap on top of her elaborate black wig. As tradition decreed, the bride's horns were supposed to be hiding underneath. Chizuko looked like a complete stranger, which she actually was.

There was the day of the ceremony, but there was also the official date on their family registry. And then there was the day they flew on Pan Am from Tokyo to Los Angeles. There were too many dates to keep track of, too many years of regret and adjustment. They found that it was better not to recognize a wedding anniversary, no reminders that they might have had a choice in the matter. It was better to pretend that they were destined to be married, and it was their job to stay that way for the rest of their lives.

★ ★ ★

This birthday, which would have been Chizuko's seventy-fifth, was a different one. Riding in the Impala's passenger seat was Genessee, who looked out the window toward the street vendors selling grilled sausages, tacos, and clothing.

Mas and Genessee kept their conversation light. They spoke about Genessee's grandson, his grandson, anything but where they were heading to.

"I'zu stop at the Yamadas today," Mas said.

"Oh?"

"Lil stay home."

"I'm so sorry about that. I think she'll regret it."

She already does, Mas thought, but he said nothing about that. It was between mother and daughter, and it was their job to figure it out.

Once he turned into the driveway for Evergreen Cemetery, Genessee became quiet. She'd never been to the historic cemetery, despite living in Los Angeles for so many decades. It wasn't like the ones advertised on billboards along the 710 and 605 Freeways. There were no promises of fish ponds or European-style chapels. The grass was even getting a brown tinge along the sides, like a cake that had been in the oven too long.

Mas looked for the statue of the Nisei soldier—it was like the needle of a compass. It grounded him, and from there he could find Chizuko's gravesite.

They parked along the driveway. Mas opened the trunk to retrieve stems of Chizuko's cymbidium. He chose the younger ones, the ones with tight, waxy faces. The cemetery didn't have a weekly throwaway policy, so there was a chance those blooms could remain for a while. He handed the flowers, wrapped in old pages of *The Rafu Shimpo*, to Genessee, and threw some rags and small pruning shears into an empty plastic bucket. Before they walked to the gravesite, Mas removed the rags and shears and filled the bucket with water from a faucet next to the walkway. There'd been a few dead leaves in the bottom of the bucket, and they swirled in the water.

They trudged to the spot, making sure they didn't step on the faces of other gravesite markers. Mas recognized many of the names they passed. Cousins, aunts, uncles, and parents of fellow gardeners, or the gardeners themselves. One day, Mas knew, his name would be cast here in metal, too.

He knelt down and began cleaning Chizuko's marker with a rag.

Genessee, still holding onto the flowers wrapped in newspaper, studied the marker. "Her birthday is today?"

Mas rubbed extra hard on the letters. Dirt tended to get stuck in between them.

She knelt on the grass next to Mas. She held onto his hands so he could not keep cleaning. "Why didn't you tell me?"

Mas couldn't say. Maybe if he said it out loud, he couldn't contain himself?

"I don't want you to erase her. I can't let go of Paul. His DNA is in our children. Our grandchildren. You can tell me anything about her, Mas. I want to hear your stories."

Mas doubted that he would say much about Chizuko, at least directly. But she was hiding there, in every moment in his past in Altadena. To attempt to carve her completely out would be impossible, or perhaps even life-threatening, to Mas.

He flipped over the cylindrical metal flower holder that had been turned upside down. The pouring of the water, the clip of the shears, and then the positioning of the cymbidium.

Would this be a funny place to propose to a woman? Mas wondered.

He must have had a strange look on his face, because Genessee quickly stood up, saying that she had to go throw the newspaper away.

Chapter Sixteen

When Mas went to pick Yuki up at the Bonaventure the next morning, the journalist was waiting with two large paper cups of coffee. The parking attendant opened the door for Yuki, who offered one of the hot cups to Mas. "Black, *desho*?" Yuki asked. "I didn't think you took your coffee with anything extra."

Mas was impressed to get something—even a cup of coffee—from the boy.

"I read Kanzo Hirose's manuscript last night," Yuki said, pulling out his digital tablet from his bag. "It's in English, so it was a little difficult for me to get through it."

His coffee squished next to the emergency brake, Mas pulled out of the Bonaventure driveway onto Grand Avenue.

"But at the end, guess what? There was an afterword by Itai-*san*."

"*Eigo*?"

"Yeah, all in English. His English wasn't bad, especially his written English. Let me read it to you."

At the stoplight, Mas took a big sip of the coffee, which

burned his tongue.

"Afterword. By Tomo Itai," Yuki began reading. "Kanzo Hirose was my uncle, one of the closest relatives I ever had. I wasn't related to him by blood, but by marriage. The most important thing about my Uncle Kanzo is that he gave me a love for baseball.

"I thought it was only a sport from the United States, but he corrected me. He taught me that baseball is more than a sport. It is a rhythm of life. Some people choose to go after the home runs of life, to go for the big, dramatic arcs, but Uncle Kanzo told me to look for the small plays. The plays that the fans, sometimes even the umpires, don't catch. The plays that make for a winning life.

"My uncle began to embrace baseball when he was interned in a concentration camp in the United States. It was on an Indian reservation, and when the Japanese Americans moved in, this camp became one of the largest groups of people in the whole state. Among those imprisoned was a man named Kenichi Zenimura, who was known as the father of Japanese American baseball. There in the desert, he helped establish a baseball diamond and a thirty-two-team league.

"My uncle didn't want to go on that boat, the *Gripsholm*, and later the *Teia*, but the US government said they had to.

"When they lived in Japan, they had absolutely nothing. My uncle Kanzo told me that he was most worried about his younger brother, Hideaki. To give him hope, he'd play baseball with him all day long.

"I myself have gone through hard times. Times of self-doubt and despair. But Kanzo taught me to embrace a baseball life."

"Not bad, *desho*?" Yuki said. "But Sunny never mentioned that baseball was that important to him."

"Maybe no big deal for Sunny," Mas said. "Maybe playin' baseball help the brotha more than him."

★ ★ ★

They parked in the same lot at the top of Dodger Stadium that they always did. Mas took the paper bag he'd brought.

"What's that?" Yuki asked.

"Sumptin I gotsu take care of." Yuki wasn't the only one with a job to do.

The attendance at the press conference was light. Only about a third of the former journalists they'd seen before showed up to find out who had killed their colleague. Most of them seemed to be local press, including a photographer for *The Rafu Shimpo*, who nodded a greeting to Mas.

The rest of the media must have headed home to Japan, Mas thought. Their stories had been filed, recorded, and broadcast. They were onto the next story, the next game, the next scandal.

Yuki took a seat, and Mas took the one next to him. With so few attendees, it made no sense to stand in the back.

Detective Williams, wearing a purple tie, stood in front of them, while his partner, Garibay—was he still in the same clothes?—stayed on the side.

"Thank you all for coming. We wanted to provide an update on the murder of Tomo Itai, a longtime reporter for the *Nippon Series*," said Cortez Williams.

"Yesterday we arrested a seventy-eight-year-old male, Hideaki 'Sunny' Hirose, and charged him with first-degree murder in Mr. Itai's death. Mr. Hirose is the victim's cousin. He came forward to police headquarters yesterday and gave a full confession. He apparently placed cyanide in medication that the victim was taking for high blood pressure. Mr. Hirose had worked in the jewelry business and had access to highly toxic chemicals used to polish silver, including cyanide."

"What was the motive?" a young Asian American woman in the front row asked.

"Mr. Hirose and Mr. Itai had gotten into a verbal altercation on Monday evening over a personal matter. That led to Mr. Hirose poisoning his cousin's capsules while the victim was sleeping."

No matter how many times a reporter urged Williams to reveal the "personal matter," he would not. Maybe that was the deal in securing Sunny's confession. To keep his motive under wraps.

"They didn't give us any credit," Yuki whispered in Mas's ear.

Mas was relieved that Williams didn't mention them. He didn't want to feel responsible for sending an old Nisei to jail. Maybe it was a feather in Yuki's cap, but Mas didn't want that on his conscience. While Yuki would be flying back to Japan, Mas would still be here in California, wondering how Sunny was faring in one of its prisons.

Mas heard the familiar tap-tap of high heels against the concrete floor. This time, Amika was wearing a royal blue dress.

"Oh, you're here," Yuki merely stated. He obviously wasn't thrilled to see her, but he seemed to be tolerating her more than he had in the past.

She said, "Let me give you some sisterly advice—"

"Sister?" Yuki cried out. "Don't you mean *oba*?" *Oba*, old hag, was a supreme insult to a woman in her forties.

"Don't be an asshole," she said. "First of all, don't worry about what the public says about the media. They need to be furious at someone, so it might as well be us. Don't forget that, Kimura-*kun*. Never sacrifice your ethics. Maybe the readers will hate you. Even your colleagues sometimes. But you can't worry about that."

Amika put her hands on her hips and leaned toward Yuki. "By the way, we didn't have sex that night. You're a total lightweight. Two drinks and you were out."

"And you," Amika said to Mas. "I will really miss you. Maybe I'll see you around someday. Maybe in Japan."

Don't count on it, Mas thought. "*Chotto*, I'zu one question for you."

"Yes." She leaned back on her heels.

"Whyzu Itai scared of Sawada?" He described how Itai cowered when Sawada challenged him on the field on that first day of the World Baseball Classic.

"Oh, that?" Amika said, smiling. "Sawada's father was a sportswriter, too. He was Itai's *senpai*."

★ ★ ★

Smitty Takaya hadn't been at the press conference. Maybe he knew that attendance would be limited to the third- and fourth-string journalists. Smitty seemed savvy about how to best spend his time.

Mas made his way to the front office. There were a couple of receptionists sitting at a curved desk, but as Mas approached, Smitty happened to be walking through the wide corridor with a walkie-talkie in his hand.

"Well hello, Mas. You were at the press conference, I figure." He signaled for Mas to follow him. They went out the door and down some stairs toward the left field pavilion. "Terrible about Itai's cousin being responsible," Smitty said. "Shocking, even."

"You knowsu Itai before?"

"Knew him well enough. I guess anyone in baseball dealing with Japan has crossed paths with Tomo Itai."

They walked inside the stadium. Smitty spoke into the walkie-talkie and waited for a response. Mas, meanwhile, opened up the paper bag he was carrying and dumped the contents onto one of the wooden benches. The decimated baseball, its guts hanging out like rolls of gauze bandages.

After responding to a message on his walkie-talkie, Smitty frowned at the mess. "What's this?"

Mas picked up the leather casing with the Japanese baseball commissioner's signature. "Dis ball from Japan."

Smitty barely glanced at the signature. "Yup."

"Youzu have one just like it."

"I do?"

"Youzu show me first time I meetcha."

Mas pointed down on the field. "There, the day Itai died."

"I guess I may have."

"Sumptin wrong with dis ball, but then you knowsu about dat."

"What do you want from me? I don't have any money, if that's what you're after."

Mas grimaced. Just what did this big-shot baseball executive think he was?

"Tomo thought there was something wrong with these new balls that the Japanese league was going to use," Smitty said. "He brought over about a dozen of them; he wanted me to check them out. I gave them to Zahed to try at practice, and yeah, they were lively. Too lively, in fact."

"So whatchu gonna do?"

"There's not much I can do. This is Japan's business, not mine. Tomo was the one who was taking them to task."

"You'zu gonna just keep your mouth shut?"

"What do you think, Mas? I know we're cut from the same cloth. Don't want to make waves, right? I've also kept my head down and have done what's been expected of me. A hundred and ten percent." Smitty glanced at his watch. "Listen, I have to cut some checks. I don't want anyone having to wait for their money."

Mas didn't move. "Youzu don't seem happy about Jin-Won being pitcha here."

Smitty, again, looked taken aback. Realizing that Mas

wasn't going to budge without a response, he finally said, "I mean, it's fine for the overseas leagues, if they want those kinds of circus acts. But what we want is power pitchers who can throw a ball at one hundred miles an hour. The public doesn't want to watch knuckleball pitches. They're too unpredictable."

Mas sighed inside. The fastest always seemed to win. That's the way it was, in baseball as in life.

★ ★ ★

As Mas was leaving, he looked down on the field. No wonder the executives wanted offices right at this angle. The way the sun hit it, the grass shined like a carpet of green emeralds.

Mas took the elevator to the field level, just to get his head back on straight. Itai's job was to dig, dig, and dig. For years, Mas's job had been to fill those holes with seeds and plants. Digging, frankly, always made Mas's head ache. Maybe it was time to give up digging for good.

He walked the dirt sidelines, admiring even the placement of the chalk. And then, appearing out of nowhere like an angel, was Uno-*san,* sitting in the dugout. Mas blinked his eyes hard, wondering if he was seeing things. He was wearing a regular sweatsuit and no baseball cap. But there was no mistaking those high cheekbones and angular chin. What was the superstar *senshu* doing here? The players from Japan had all left days ago.

Mas couldn't help but take a few steps forward.

"*Konnichiwa*," Uno-*san* said to him.

How did he know that Mas could speak Japanese?

Mas saw a canister of some kind of cleanser next to Uno-*san* on the bench. He was rubbing his mitt with a rag, and Mas noticed that his cleats were also on the bench.

"*Osoji*," Uno-*san* said. Cleaning.

Mas was tongue-tied. His legs were frozen in place. He couldn't escape even if he wanted to.

"You like playing in America?" Mas asked in Japanese. A *bakatare* comment, but it was the first thing to come to his lips.

"Sah, the stadiums are all a little different. Not all the same like in Japan." Uno-*san* then put his mitt down and admired the field. "Beauty of America, *ne*. Real, natural grass."

THE END

Acknowledgments

First of all, thanks to Kimiko Ego, who was the first one to tell me of the Japanese-style garden at Dodger Stadium. *Domo arigato.* If it weren't for you, *Sayonara Slam* probably never would have come to be.

This book is one of my most heavily researched mysteries. The scholarship of Japanese and Japanese Americans in baseball has been taken up by a number of academicians and experts. Robert Whiting is likely the most well-known in terms of baseball in Japan. His *You Gotta Have Wa* and *The Meaning of Ichiro: The New Wave from Japan and the Transformation of Our National Pastime* both proved helpful. To get into the head of a Japanese baseball superstar, in particular Ichiro, I was assisted by the DVD produced by Bandai, *Ichiro x Takeshi Kyatchiboru Seisaku,* and by the book *Ichiro on Ichiro: Conversations with Narumi Komatsu.* Robert K. Fitts's *Remembering Japanese Baseball: An Oral History of the Game* provided firsthand perspectives of Japanese Americans playing professional ball in Japan.

I've been a fan of the lifelong work of Kerry Yo Nakagawa ever since I worked at *The Rafu Shimpo* newspaper. His *Japanese American Baseball in California: A History* was a notable reference for this book. Also beneficial was Samuel O. Regalado's *Nikkei Baseball: Japanese American Players from Immigration and Internment to the Major Leagues.*

Dodger Stadium is a character in itself. Thanks to the Dodger docents; I highly recommend that history and sports lovers take a tour of the stadium. Kimiko Ego kindly lent me history books written by Dodger historian Mark Langill, as well as her personal collection of clippings of the *ishi doro* (stone lantern) that was donated by Japanese sportwriter Sotaro Suzuki in 1965 and rededicated in 2003. (Langill also clarified where the greenskeepers' equipment storage would be located.) And Cultural Clash's "Chavez Ravine: A Revival" presented the darker side of the stadiuim's establishment.

Two exhibitions—the Ronald Reagan Presidential Library's "Baseball! The Exhibition" and the Japanese American National Museum's "Dodgers: Brotherhood of the Game"—were filled with historic photographs and memorabilia that aided in envisioning the Dodgers' past.

For the international aspects of the book, I referred to "'Koreans, Go Home!' Internet Nationalism in Contemporary Japan as a Digitally Meditated Subculture" in *The Asia-Pacific Journal: Japan Focus*; Karen Colligan-Taylor's translation of Tomoko Yamazaki's *Sandakan Brothel No. 8: An Episode in the History of Lower-Class Japanese Women*; Caroline Elkins's *Settler Colonialism in the Twentieth Century: Projects, Practices, Legacies*; Monica Kim's article, "Empire's Babel: US Military Interrogation Rooms of the Korean War"; Jan Jarboe Russell's *The Train to Crystal City: FDR's Secret Prisoner Exchange Program and America's Only Family Internment Camp During World War II*; and Atsushi "Archie" Miyamoto's manuscript, "The *Gripsholm* Exchanges: A Short Concise Report on the Exchange of Hostages during World War II Between the United States and Japan as it Relates to Japanese Americans." (Appreciation goes out to Thomas Philo of the Cal State Dominguez Hills Archives.)

For anyone who wants to know the mysterious ways of

a knuckleball pitcher, I heartily recommend the Ricki Stern and Annie Sundberg documentary *Knuckleball!* R.A. Dickey's memoir, *Wherever I Wind Up: My Quest for Truth, Authenticity, and the Perfect Knuckleball*, is a great read, too.

Answering a call for various bits of information were Mark Schreiber, Coleen Nakamura, Komo Gauvreau, Todd Leighley, Bobby Okinaka, Richard Kondo, Kenji Nakano, J.K. Yamamoto, Lauren Xerxes, and Kay Hadashi.

For a more personal perspective, I learned much from La Vida de Izumi's YouTube videos, as well as meeting Grandma Lee in Los Angeles, compliments of Kathy Masaoka of Nikkei for Civil Rights and Redress.

Thanks to the support of Judd and Leslie Matsunaga for the Yonsei Basketball Association and their purchase of the naming rights to two characters, Smitty Takaya and April Sue. Of course, the real people bear little resemblance to the fictional characters in *Sayonara Slam*.

Mary Cannon and Sherry Kanzer lent their eagle eyes to identify some minor corrections. My thanks to both women for their support of Mas and my writing career.

And finally, again, kudos to my agent, Allison Cohen, and to Colleen Dunn Bates, publisher of Prospect Park Books, for her commitment to books set in Los Angeles. She, book designer Amy Inouye, marketing associate Caitlin Ek, and proofreader Margery Schwartz make the whole crazy and ever-changing business of publishing a true joy.

Acknowledgments, as always, end with my husband, Wes, who helped me parse out the details involving knuckleballs, baseball strategy, and sports stadiums. The love of the game continues.

About the Author

Naomi Hirahara is the Edgar Award–winning author of the Mas Arai mystery series. Also nominated for the Macavity and Anthony awards, the series includes *Strawberry Yellow, Blood Hina, Snakeskin Shamisen, Gasa-Gasa Girl,* and *Summer of the Big Bachi.* She is also the author of the Ellie Rush mystery series, as well as *1001 Cranes,* a novel for children. A graduate of Stanford University, Hirahara has also written many nonfiction books about gardening and Japanese American history and culture. Learn more at naomihirahara.com.